Love is Beautiful Book 1

New Adult Sweet Romance Series, Volume 5

Ellie J. Adams

Published by Wheelhouse Publishers LLC, 2020.

Copyright

Pittsfield, MA 01201
To learn more about Wheelhouse Publishers, visit:
wheelhousepublishers.com

Chapter 1

Amber Holloway felt faint as she raced across the lush, green lawn of the main campus of Higgins College. Her first day of class and she had overslept. Reaching the end of the perfectly manicured grass, she swerved left, panting heavily as she jogged up the concrete walkway that led to the Fine Arts Building. Finally, she stood by the thick glass doors, leaning over to catch her breath. A wave of dizziness overtook her. She sank to the ground as everything faded to black.

"Whoa! Are you okay?" The warm voice above her sounded as though it was traveling down a tunnel.

Strong arms lifted her up and she collapsed against a muscular, lean chest that smelled faintly of turpentine and paint.

When she finally opened her eyes, she found a face inches from her own. Beautiful green eyes stared down at her. The boy holding her could have popped off the cover of *GQ* Magazine, in spite of his paint-spattered tee-shirt and jeans. His glossy dark hair was fashionably unkempt. A day of stubble darkened his cheeks. His skin was an exotic honey tone.

"Can I get you something?"

"Sugar," Amber said. "Need sugar." She closed her eyes against the next bout of nausea.

"Wait here and I'll grab something from the vending machine."

The boy shifted and Amber found herself propped against the hard brick building. She heard the thud of his steps and the clank of the door opening and shutting.

She felt the fog of low blood sugar settling back over her like a damp blanket. What if the boy didn't return?

And then the door clanked again.

"Hey, I'm back."

She heard the crack of a soda can opening and the fizz of carbonation. A firm hand cradled her neck and tilted her head back.

"Here, take a sip of this."

A cold can pressed against her lips.

Amber greedily took a big gulp of syrupy sweet soda. She could feel the sugar powering through her. She took another sip. And then another. The murky fog started to recede.

She sighed and opened her eyes.

"Thanks. I overslept and didn't have time to eat."

The boy didn't need to know that dinner the previous night was a single packet of noodles. She had scraped together some loose change to buy a candy bar from the vending machines after class.

"Diabetes?" The boy's forehead wrinkled with concern.

"Just low blood sugar. I'll be okay in a few minutes. This soda definitely helped."

To prove her point, she struggled to get to her feet.

"Give yourself a little time. Class can wait."

The boy took her hand and sat next to her.

Amber recovered enough to feel a tingle go through her from the boy's rough hand. Was her own hand sweaty? Would he notice? She needed to say something. Anything.

"I can't believe I'm late for my first class."

The boy looked straight into her eyes. The effect was mesmerizing.

"I bet the instructor will understand. Who do you have?"

Amber scrunched her face up, trying to clear her head. The boy's captivating eyes and rough hand distracted her. His body was close enough that she smelled the shampoo he must have used that morning. She suspected the tingling she felt had nothing to do with the sugar buzzing through her system.

"Collins," she said at last.

"Perfect!" The boy grinned. "I'm the TA for that class. Ben is cool."

Amber stared at his red full lips, slowly realizing how she had left the apartment. In the next instant, she was assessing herself with a growing sense of horror. She hadn't had time for a shower and was wearing the same jeans and tee-shirt from the day before. Had she even brushed her hair?

"My name's Hunter, by the way. Hunter Webb."

Amber nodded numbly and sipped at the soda.

"Are you sure you're okay?"

Amber nodded again, this time more vigorously. She smiled.

"Um . . . Can you tell me your name?" Hunter stared at her as though she had brain damage.

Oh! Amber felt the blood rushing up her face and neck. She must look like a lunatic.

"Oh, yeah, sorry. I'm Amber Holloway."

Shaking her head, she fought against the last wisps of dizziness and struggled to her feet. This time, Hunter helped her up and gathered up her bag of art supplies.

"I can walk by myself," she muttered weakly.

As they started down the long corridor, Amber spotted an unfamiliar girl frowning at her. Weird.

"Are you sure you're okay?" Hunter paused and peered down at her anxiously.

Amber wanted to spend all day staring into those gorgeous emerald eyes.

Hunter refused to let her go, one arm steadying her as they walked through the halls. She tried to pull away once more as they entered the large classroom. But Hunter just gripped her arm more firmly and led her to a seat in the front row.

"Sorry we're late, Ben," he remarked. "This is Amber Holloway. She felt a bit sick on the way, but I think she's going to be just fine."

"Sorry to hear that, Amber. Welcome to class. If you need to leave early, just let Hunter know. I'm sure he would be happy to escort you home or to the infirmary."

Professor Collins was a slender man, dressed in faded denim jeans and a black tee-shirt. He blended in with the class, looking even hipper than some of his students. Wavy blond hair was swept to one side. He wore black framed glasses that made him look cool rather than nerdy.

"Thanks," Amber whispered, certain that every eye in the class was on her.

Staring past the instructor, she thought she saw a girl's face looking through the small window in the classroom door. The same girl as before? Amber shook her head and blinked. When she looked again, the girl's face was gone. Her low blood sugar must be making her see things.

Professor Collins handed her a syllabus and turned back to the class.

"Class, Hunter Webb will be my TA this semester. He's a junior and has already taken most of my courses. He can help you with technique and will be leading a few of the classes as well. You will find his e-mail and cell phone contacts in your syllabus."

Several students (mostly female) whipped out cell phones to enter Hunter's information. Amber forced herself to stop staring at Hunter and focus on Professor Collins.

"As you know, this class focuses on human anatomy. Starting tomorrow, we will be using live models. If anyone is interested in being a model for this or any other class, please let Hunter know and he can give you the details."

The announcement left Amber a little anxious. She struggled with human faces. She suspected most of her classmates had more experience. Her drawing skills were amateurish for somebody who wanted to major in art. Even though she had always liked to draw as a teen, her high school work-study program hadn't left much time for extracurricular activities. She had taken her first couple of basic art courses at a community college the year before.

Hunter maneuvered around the room, passing out supplies. He moved with such ease, almost carelessly. His jeans, cinched with a worn leather belt, emphasized a narrow waist. Flustered, Amber stared at her desk. But when she peeked up again, she noticed that almost every other female in the room was also following Hunter's every move.

Professor Collins cleared his throat dramatically and pointed at a table at the front of the room.

"I've put together a small still life. Since I don't know many of you, I would like to see what skills you are bringing to class. Show me any techniques you've acquired from other classes or on your own."

"Still feel okay?"

Startled, Amber looked up to find Hunter's face inches from her own. She held up her finished soda can.

"Thanks to the magic potion." She smiled with frozen lips.

"Great, but stay put after class. I'm going to walk you back to your dorm."

"That's not necessary!"

But Hunter simply slapped down a piece of drawing paper and a charcoal pencil and moved on.

Amber was still working when she raised her head and realized that most of the students had already left. At the front of the room, a curvy brunette spoke to Hunter. Wait, was that the same girl from the hallway?

Hunter spoke quietly and then shook his head firmly. He seemed annoyed. The girl stormed out of the classroom.

Looking around, Amber noted that she was the only one to see the interaction. Professor Collins was deep in conversation with a student at the back of the room. She supposed it was really none of her business. Bending her head, Amber got back to her drawing.

"Good job, Amber."

She glanced up as though waking from a dream. Wow. Just looking at him took her breath away. She fought an urge to run her fingers through that thick mass of tussled hair.

Okay, stay focused, Amber. This isn't like you. You don't fall for boys you've just met.

"Thanks," Amber said shyly. She appraised her work. "But something doesn't feel right about the vase."

Hunter knelt next to her. He held up a finger and squinted at the still life.

Amber felt her stomach flutter as his arm brushed against hers.

"The proportion is slightly off."

Hunter reached out and picked up her right hand.

Amber felt a warm tingle from his warm, rough skin. It was ridiculous that Hunter was having this affect on her.

"Use your finger as a measuring stick," Hunter instructed, his face so close to hers that she felt his warm breath on her face.

A shiver shot up Amber's spine.

"See how your fingernail is about the size of that apple?"

Almost immediately, Amber did see. She glanced down at her drawing and realized that the vase she had drawn was shorter than it should have been.

"I know how to fix it," she said, her voice sounding breathy.

Hunter released her hand but made no effort to move away. His face was still so close she could smell the mint from his toothpaste. She felt herself flushing and had to concentrate hard to pick up the charcoal and make the changes. With a few strokes, the symmetry finally felt right.

"Excellent!" Hunter announced, standing abruptly. "I just need to talk to Ben for a minute and then I'll walk you back."

The change in mood was so sudden that Amber wondered what had happened. She was sure that she had not imagined the electricity between them. She glanced around the room and then froze.

The girl had returned. She frowned at Amber.

Twisting, Amber saw that Hunter was engrossed in conversation with Professor Collins.

The girl wandered carelessly around the room, pretending to admire sketches tacked to the classroom walls. But like a predator, she circled closer to Amber. She picked up a paintbrush, clenching it in one hand.

She looked like she would be happy to stab Amber with it.

Chapter 2

I haven't done anything wrong, Amber thought fiercely. She forced herself to sit up straight and smile. She had long ago learned that the best way to deal with aggressors was to pretend like she was not affected.

The busty girl narrowed her eyes and marched up to Amber.

"You don't look very sick to me," she said, her voice low but icy.

Amber clenched her charcoal in sweaty palms.

"I'm feeling much better. Thanks for asking."

She held out her hand. "I'm Amber. I just transferred this year."

The girl ignored her hand. She stuck her face right into Amber's personal space. Her coffee breath was an assault weapon.

"Listen up, Amber. My name is Kayla. But the only thing you need to know about me is that Hunter is my boyfriend. So keep your grubby little hands off him."

Oh! Hunter was dating this girl! Amber's ears burned. This was so embarrassing.

"Look, Kayla. I had no idea . . ."

She broke off as Hunter, face glowering, stepped between the two girls.

"What's going on, Kayla? Why are you here?"

Kayla lost her impervious look. She put an arm around Amber's shoulder.

"I thought I dropped my bracelet earlier this morning. I was searching for it when I saw this girl looking as though she might faint."

Kayla's fingers dug into Amber's skin.

"I . . . um . . . I . . ." Amber stammered.

Hunter's face instantly melted into concern.

"That's it. I'm taking you back to your dorm right now."

Hunter turned to Kayla. "Thanks, but I've got it from here."

"But I could walk her back!" Kayla exclaimed, realizing her error.

"No can do," Hunter announced. "If she passes out, there's no way you could carry her."

"But . . ." Kayla's eyes flashed and Amber knew the girl was scheming to change the events.

But Hunter had already scooped Amber up in his arms and was heading for the door.

"Let Ben know I'll see him later, okay?"

Hunter didn't wait for a response.

Amber was so shocked to be in Hunter's arms for the second time that day that it took her a moment to collect her thoughts.

"I'm sure this isn't necessary."

Amber tried to put some conviction in her voice.

Her conscience blasted her.

What? You are actually enjoying this? Getting carted around like a helpless infant?

Amber told her conscience to get lost. She wasn't doing anything wrong. It wasn't like she was trying to steal Kayla's boyfriend. And she really did feel woozy and lightheaded.

In fact, she was so weak that she simply settled against Hunter's warm chest. This must be a dream. Cuddling against his body was not exactly a hardship.

Ordinarily, this act would have annoyed her. Amber was not some silly girl looking for Prince Charming. She had grown up having to take care of herself.

Surprisingly, though, Amber felt comfortable in Hunter's arms. Okay, more than comfortable. So much so that her conscience attacked once more.

What happened to being strong and independent? What kind of modern day woman lets a guy carry her around like a trophy.

Amber felt the steady thump of Hunter's heart where their bodies pressed together. She inhaled soap and turpentine. She told her conscience to back off.

Most guys had little effect on Amber. But Hunter was different. Those glittering green eyes hypnotized her. His touch buzzed through her body like a current of electricity. Even his hand brushing her arm in art class had left her breathless. And now this.

Her conscience slipped back in and berated her.

Get a grip! He has a girlfriend. A pretty girlfriend who could pass as a model. You'd better be more concerned with how you're going to eat in the next few days.

As though to taunt her, Amber's stomach growled. She thought of the few packs of noodles in her kitchen cabinet. If the student loan money didn't come in the next couple of days, she wasn't sure how she was going to buy groceries or pay the rent.

At her apartment door, Hunter demanded the key and Amber fished it from a string she carried around her neck. Inside, he lowered her onto the single camping mattress on the floor of the tiny apartment.

Amber rolled onto her side, squeezing her eyes against the bout of dizziness and nausea. She heard Hunter rummaging in the kitchen, opening cabinet after cabinet and slamming the refrigerator shut. She tried to prop her head up but was simply too tired. Whatever adrenaline had kept her going in art class had evaporated.

Amber heard Hunter come into the room, but he didn't say anything. She felt too ill to open her eyes. She listened to his footsteps moving back into the kitchen and then his low voice. Was he speaking to her? No, it sounded as though he was on the phone.

Hunter opened the refrigerator door again.

Amber stifled a hysterical laugh. Did Hunter honestly think more food would mysteriously appear if he kept opening the door? As if in response to her thought, the fridge door slammed shut.

Moments later, the cheap inflatable mattress lurched as Hunter sank beside her. If she wasn't feeling so sick, she would be horrified at him seeing her meager belongings like this.

Amber nearly gasped out loud as Hunter's warm fingers slid beneath her hair and cradled her neck. He gently propped her against his chest.

"Open your mouth."

A spoon clicked against her lower teeth and slid against Amber's tongue. The sweetness of strawberry jam jolted her senses. She sighed as the sugar took the edge off her dizziness.

When she had licked the spoon clean, Hunter fed her more jam as though she were a baby. She felt ashamed of her helplessness, but let him feed her like that until she could open her eyes.

When she dared to peek up at him, Amber was startled to find that he looked angry.

"Are you anorexic?" A vein throbbed in Hunter's neck.

"What? No! What makes you think that?"

Amber stared up at him in confusion. The absurdity of it finally got to her. She started to giggle hysterically. Soon, she was alternating between giggling and sobbing.

"Shh! It's okay." Hunter shifted so that he was now cradling her in his arms.

He ran one thumb over her cheek and stared down at her.

"You're hyperventilating. You need to calm down."

Amber couldn't help it. Another fit of laughing overtook her, causing her stomach to ache. But before she could even catch her breath, she was sobbing once more.

Hunter leaned down. His lips parted as though about to kiss her.

And then, without thinking, Amber felt drawn to move her face closer. Hunter's eyes widened with surprise. He pulled away, his movements sudden and abrupt.

"I'm sorry, Amber. I didn't mean to take advantage of you." He blushed. "I was just trying to . . ."

Amber flushed, the blood surging from her neck all the way to her scalp. She had wanted him to kiss her.

Her conscience flared.

What the world are you doing, Amber? You can't be kissing another girl's boyfriend. No matter how handsome he is. No matter how much he takes your breath away.

At least the shock of the almost kiss had stunned her out of hyperventilating. She sat up awkwardly. Even now, in spite of the shame, she still felt attracted to Hunter. Having him so close in class was going to kill her.

A loud knock broke the tension.

Hunter scrambled to his feet and hurried to the door. Seconds later, he grabbed a bag from another guy in the hallway. Even from where she was sitting, Amber could smell Chinese food. She heard the guys speaking in low voices before Hunter returned.

"That was my roommate bringing over leftovers from last night," Hunter called out as he rummaged in the kitchen cabinets.

"He heated everything at our place since you don't seem to have a microwave."

Finding the one bowl Amber owned, Hunter dumped half the container in and grabbed a spoon.

In spite of her watering mouth, Amber wanted to refuse. But her stomach chose that moment to growl so loudly that Hunter started to laugh. When Hunter handed her the bowl, she couldn't make herself slow down. When she had shoveled half the sweet and sour chicken into her stomach, she remembered he was watching.

"When was the last time you ate?"

"Yesterday." She couldn't face him. "I couldn't eat this morning because . . . "

"You overslept," Hunter said, finishing her sentence.

Amber blushed. Oh, right, he's seen your empty cabinet and refrigerator.

Hunter glanced around the tiny, studio apartment.

"No pictures of family?"

Amber laughed harshly.

"We don't exactly get along."

She waved her hand at the bare walls. "I haven't had time to decorate."

Or money. But that was probably obvious by now.

"Roommate?"

"Never showed up."

Amber sighed and closed her eyes. She had gotten stuck paying the deposit when the girl bailed on her.

Hunter took her bowl and filled it with vegetable fried rice.

Amber wanted to cry because it tasted so good. She didn't look up again until she had scraped the bowl clean. When she did, Hunter handed her two wrapped fortune cookies.

"This must look kind of messed up, huh?"

He looked out of place in her barren apartment.

Hunter chuckled.

"Why would I think that? Because you sleep on an inflatable camping mattress? Don't have furniture? Or because you have no food and seem half-starved?"

Amber sighed. "My student loans should be here any day now."

Hunter regarded her thoughtfully and then looked down as his phone beeped.

"I've got to get going. I have class in fifteen minutes. What about you?"

Pawing through an untidy pile of papers beside the mattress, Amber found her schedule.

"I don't have another class until one o'clock."

Hunter stood and Amber realized that she was sad to see him leave. After today, his girlfriend Kayla would make sure that she never saw him again outside of art class.

"Thanks for today. I had no idea that my blood sugar was so low this morning. I would probably still be comatose in front of the art building if you hadn't come by when you did."

Hunter cupped her chin in his hand.

"Never fear. I'm going to officially be keeping an eye on you from here on out."

He grinned. "And that's a promise."

With one more quick look at his phone, Hunter gave her a small salute and left.

Grinning, Amber grabbed some clean clothes and headed for the shower. Kayla or no Kayla, the next time Hunter saw her, she was going to look her best.

Chapter 3

Amber's History professor droned on in a monotone voice, leaving half the class yawning into their fists. Amber's cheap flip phone didn't have a record function, so she was stuck taking notes.

The jock sitting next to her didn't even pretend to pay attention. He was sound asleep and leaving a disgusting pile of drool over the top of his desk. Most of the other students appeared to be surfing the web or texting. Only a few students at the front laughed at the instructor's lame jokes. Amber figured they must be history majors.

When the professor gave the class a ten minute break, she used the time to check her banking balance. Seventeen dollars and fifty-six cents. Yikes! Another rent payment was due the following week. And she still hadn't paid for this month yet. Her wallet held twenty-two dollars. If she thought about it any more, she was going to be sick. She had to get a job. Any job.

After the break, Amber focused all her attention on history. Even a boring lecture was more pleasant than worrying about her money problems.

After class, Amber stood in line yet again so that she could ask about her student loan. Every time she checked online, she got a message saying her loan was "still processing." Once again, she wasted twenty minutes of her time as the student worker told her that the checks had not been released.

"We can give you an emergency loan against your loan," the girl said sympathetically.

"Does it cost anything?" Amber asked wearily.

"Just fifteen percent interest," the girl answered cheerfully.

Amber gasped. "You mean the school charges fifteen percent interest on money that I am already paying an origination fee and interest on?"

The girl shrugged.

"Sorry, but that's what it is. Are you interested or not?" She looked pointedly at the students lined up behind Amber.

"Not today," Amber said, forcing herself to remain calm. Getting angry at a student worker wasn't going to change anything.

Walking home, she felt desperate. She didn't have transportation to get to the mall for a job. She had applied too late to get a work-study job. She slammed the door to her apartment and slumped on the blowup mattress. The uneaten fortune cookies flew up in the air.

At least she had gotten in one decent meal today. That was something to be grateful for.

Her cell phone rang and startled her. She saw the caller and smiled. If anybody could make her feel better, it was her best friend.

"Hannah! How are you?"

She listened as Hannah filled her in on her classes at an out-of-state college. Both girls attended the same community college the year before. Hannah lacked the grades to get in anywhere else. Amber had lacked the money to go elsewhere.

But as soon as Heather's grades improved, she immediately transferred. She begged Amber to go with her. But all the nagging in the world couldn't improve Amber's finances. Even Higgins College was a stretch.

In spite of scrimping and saving to attend Higgins College, a relatively affordable public school, Amber felt guilty. In the past, she had helped Hannah write more than a few class papers. She knew Hannah was going to struggle to keep up. So now she gave Hannah news she wanted to hear.

"So I met this guy named Hunter."

Hannah didn't need to know that the guy had a girlfriend. For now, Amber just wanted to feed her best friend some good news.

"What?!" Hannah squealed from her end of the phone. "Tell me all about him."

Amber carefully related information, careful to avoid any talk of her money issues. Finally, she realized she was running low on her minutes. She couldn't afford a monthly plan and had to rely on phone cards.

"Hey, I have get going for my next class."

Did you just lie to your best friend? She would understand if you told her about the money situation. Wouldn't she?

"Just be safe with that new guy," Hannah said and laughed. "Remember everything that my Dad taught us. You don't have me to kick butt for you anymore."

As she hung up, Amber guiltily wondered how they had managed to stay best friends all these years. The two were so different from each other. Heather was the party girl, flitting from guy to guy as quickly and as easily as she might go through magazines. Amber was the studious one, always staying up late to get good grades. When she wasn't studying, she had worked at a fast food restaurant to save money for college.

Amber's conscious grew indignant.

How can you even think that? Heather's family has always been there for you. Sure, Hannah sometimes takes advantage of you. But you owe her. Where else would you have gone when your mom flew into drunken rages or disappeared for days on end with all the grocery money?

Being friends with Hannah had also helped Amber survive advances from her mother's sleazy boyfriends. Hannah's Dad was a martial arts trainer and had taught the girls how to defend themselves at a young age. By the time she was sixteen, Amber had been able to knock more than one arrogant drunk on his behind.

Of course, that hadn't made Amber's mother look upon her daughter any more favorably. She was convinced that Amber was trying to steal her boyfriends.

As she let the crispy fortune cookies melt on her tongue, Amber shook away images of her former life. She had to clear her head. Shoving her feet into her sneakers, she decided to take a walk around campus.

The canopy of trees over the sidewalks made her feel like she was on a movie set. But the idyllic setting failed to assuage her anxiety about finances. If anything, she saw how much she stood to lose. More than anything, she didn't want to have to give all of this up. She returned to her apartment, determined to spend the evening look for job opportunities.

She sweated as she climbed the four flights of stairs. She stared at the peeling paint and grimy carpets in the hallway. What had gone through Hunter's mind when he carried her through here?

Someone had left a paper bag in front of her door. Puzzled, Amber opened it up. Inside she found a quart of orange juice, a pint of milk, a carton of eggs, a loaf of bread, a fork, and a small bowl of butter. A folded note was taped on top of the bowl. *I'll be at your place promptly at 8 am for breakfast. Mix an egg or two into your noodles tonight for a more filling dinner. – Hunter.*

Amber's conscience kicked into overdrive.

He has a girlfriend. This means nothing. Thank him with a polite e-mail but turn him down for the breakfast.

Amber read the note five times. She banished her conscience, carried the groceries inside, and started her noodles.

Was it okay to allow somebody's boyfriend to buy her food? Her conscience said no. Her stomach said yes.

Was it okay to daydream about kissing somebody else's boyfriend. Again, her conscience said no while her heart said yes.

Could she stop Hunter from thinking he was responsible for carting her around every time she fainted. Did she want him to stop?

Amber told her conscience to quit bothering her.

The next morning, Amber woke with lingering dreams of Hunter's lips on her own. She quickly showered, trying to wash away the feeling. She certainly wasn't going to try to take somebody's boyfriend. She would make things clear with Hunter as soon as he showed up. Say thank you very much for the food and assistance, but she was fine now.

She stopped midway shaving her leg. Oh, yeah, and also admit that she was indeed dead broke and needed a job. She laughed at the absurdity.

She finished showering and drying her hair with no clear idea of how to handle Hunter Webb. She spent so long in the bathroom that she was only half-dressed when she heard him knocking.

She started for the door and then stopped. She had almost welcomed Hunter inside while she was half naked.

"Just a second!" she yelled, yanking on clean jeans.

Grabbing a tee-shirt, she rushed to the door. She was so flustered that she tripped over her shoes and stubbed her toe on a crate of books. She howled, rolling on the floor in pain.

"Amber? Are you okay? Open the door!"

Reaching up with teary eyes, Amber unlocked the door and rolled away.

Hunter burst through the door. "What is it? Where are you hurt?"

Still moaning, Amber pointed at her throbbing toe.

"No, don't touch it!" she shrieked when he attempted to pick up her foot.

Hunter backed away, quietly watching her until the pain subsided and she could sit up. Then he reached for her foot again.

She pulled away, scowling.

"I won't touch your toe. I promise."

Hunter carefully lifted her foot. As her bare skin made contact with the warmth of his hand, she flushed. This situation was getting ridiculous. She was definitely not moving in the right direction of disengagement from another girl's boyfriend.

Hunter squinted at her reddened toe. He shook his head sadly.

"I'm sorry, Miss Holloway, but this toe is going to be hideously bruised. I'm going to have to recommend an amputation."

"Oh, stop it!" Amber giggled and slapped his shoulder.

"Let's see if you can walk." Hunter gently placed her foot on the floor and then knelt to help her up.

As they stood, Hunter's thick hair brushed against her neck and she gasped.

"I'm sorry! Did I hurt you?" Hunter abruptly lifted her so that all the weight was off her foot.

"No . . . Um . . . Maybe a little," Amber stammered. "I just need another couple of minutes before I try again."

Hunter deposited her onto the squishy mattress.

"If I didn't know any better, I would think that you were angling to get breakfast made in bed," he said teasingly.

"That was my plan. Is it working?"

Amber shifted on the mattress. Was it her imagination or was it starting to sag in the middle?

Hunter laughed.

"Yes, but that's just as well. I'm picky about how my eggs are cooked."

Amber got to her feet and hobbled forward.

"Seriously, Hunter. You don't have to cook for me."

Hunter closed the refrigerator, placed the eggs on the counter, and confronted her. Taking Amber by the shoulders, he firmly pushed her back onto the mattress.

"Seriously, I do. Now don't move again."

Amber sighed and watched him scramble the eggs. If she wasn't so hungry she would do the sensible thing and make

Hunter leave. But her growling stomach and aching toe kept her in place.

She shifted her attention to her deplorable finances. The student loan would pay her basic costs. But food, books, and art supplies were already more than she had anticipated when she transferred from the community college. And this was simply one more student loan piled onto the others. She didn't even want to contemplate how she would ever begin to pay them off once she had her degree. She knew most artists made little money.

The smell of cooking eggs brought her back to the present and made her mouth water. She crawled over to the crate of books that had led to her stumped toe. Usually she ate standing or sitting on the mattress. But the crate, flipped on its side, would make a decent table. She put a large, flat art history book on top for a makeshift tabletop before ripping out a clean sheet of drawing paper for a temporary tablecloth.

"My, my! She brings out the luxury furniture for breakfast!"

Hunter appeared, armed with a heaping plate of scrambled eggs and several slices of bread heaped with butter and jam.

"I would have toasted the bread but couldn't find any potholders for the oven."

Amber grabbed a fork and was already filling her mouth before Hunter sat down.

"I'm sorry," she said, blushing, after seeing how he was staring at her.

She shoved the plate closer to him on the makeshift table.

"I know this is for both of us."

Hunter looked as though he was about to say something. But his phone started to beep.

"We need to talk later. But let's just eat and get to class right now."

He lowered his fork and quickly ate several bites.

Amber noticed he was purposely eating less than she was. Still, she couldn't stop herself from wolfing down most of the plate. She had skipped so many meals the last few weeks to stretch her money. Her body seemed desperate to make up the loss. She ate three out of the four slices of bread and jam, shoving the last few bites in even as they left the building and started the walk toward campus.

Chapter 4

Only as they hurried to class did Amber start to worry that Kayla might show up again. What if the girl saw her walking with Hunter?

They got to class early so that Hunter could meet the woman who would be modeling for the students. A small raised platform with a lone chair had been placed at the front of the room.

Amber found her own seat and pulled out her new sketch pad and charcoal pencils. Her fingers itched to start drawing. Ever since she was a small child, she had loved to disappear into herself as she drew. It was one of the few things that brought her complete peace from her chaotic childhood.

An older woman with some gray in her hair walked hesitantly into the room. Hunter greeted her with a warm smile as the other students began spilling into the large, open classroom. Just after the final bell rang, Hunter conferred with Professor Collins, who walked in at the last minute.

Finally, Professor Collins addressed the class.

"Remember the words of John Sloan as you work. He wrote: 'The important thing to bear in mind while drawing the figure is that the model is a human being, that is alive, that exists there on the stand. Look on the model with respect. Appreciate his or her humanity. Be very humble before that human being. Be filled with wonder at its reality and life. There is a human creature that lives and breathes and feels, a being with a mind and character of its own – not a patchwork of light and shadow, color and shape.'"

Amber swallowed, feeling nervous. What Hunter thought about her drawing shouldn't matter. But it did. She wanted his approval.

Professor Collins signaled to the model that she could begin.

"As always, no speaking to or touching the model," he reminded the students.

The woman, wearing a silk dress and low heels, walked calmly to the raised platform and up the few steps. When she sat, the full skirt of the dress fell into rippling folds around her legs and ankles. She glanced at the large clock on the wall and then struck her first pose. She twisted her torso slightly and raised both arms above her head, clasping her hands together. She moved her head to one side to create a clean profile.

For the first few seconds, Amber sat transfixed. As soon as she heard the scratching of pencil on paper, however, she snapped out of her apprehension and focused on capturing the model's form. She quickly sketched in the woman's silhouette and then began to capture some of the details. Although thin, the woman's belly bulged slightly. The skin on her arms had lost elasticity. Thick blue veins lined the backs of her elegant, long hands. But she held herself with confidence and authority.

Amber was engrossed in her drawing when all too soon the woman shifted her pose. This time, she crossed her legs, shifting her hips slightly. One foot crossed the other, showing the bottom half of one muscular calf. She reached up and loosened her salt and pepper hair so that it splayed down her back. One hand reached up as though to touch her neck while the other rested on one thigh.

As Amber and her classmates worked, Professor Collins and Hunter silently circled the room, peering at sketches but not speaking. Amber sketched furiously the rest of class and was only vaguely aware of either the Professor or Hunter viewing her work. She was surprised when the model stopped and quietly left the room. An entire hour had flown by.

Professor Collins asked Hunter to pull forward a model skeleton.

"Some of you are having difficulties with proportions. I want each of you to study Mr. Bones here and make note of how each limb relates to the other in size and position. In particular, where does the hand fall in relation to the hip? Study the hands themselves. Observe the fingertip lengths. Also, make sure you check your syllabus for homework assignments this week."

Professor Collins and Hunter spent the next half hour canvassing the room and making comments on the sketches. Professor Collins nodded several times as he viewed Amber's work.

"You have a good eye," he said. "I like how you captured the lines so quickly in these. Keep an eye out on your proportions though. See how this arm is too short here? Overall, though, good work."

Amber was glowing as Professor Collins moved on to the next student. By the time class was over, Hunter was busy with several students. Oh, well, she really didn't have time to stay late today. She was anxious to get to the Financial Aid Office.

After a brief stand in line, she was happily surprised when the student worker let her know that the loan had been processed.

"Great!" Amber gushed. "Can I get a check for it?"

"The money got placed in your account," the guy said. He sounded bored. "You'll have to make an appointment to see one of the Financial Aid Officers to have some of it taken out."

"I need money right away," Amber insisted. "Can I see somebody now?"

A few minutes later, a harried woman checked over her account.

"Your classes and fees are all paid for the semester. Let me see how much you have left that can be withdrawn."

When told the amount, Amber's face fell.

"That's it?" she moaned. "That only covers my rent. Can I get more?"

"You've taken out the maximum subsidized government loan already. You can take out a private loan but you would need your parents to co-sign. I don't see any information in your file for them. Are they deceased?"

Amber was tempted to say yes, but she knew that they would only ask for proof. "No, we're just estranged," she admitted in a small voice. "I no longer have contact with either of them."

"Well, my dear, I'm sure that things can be smoothed over. Why don't you talk to them? I'm sure you can work things out."

"Thank you for your help," Amber said curtly, standing.

This always happened. Nobody wanted to believe that your parents could be anything but helpful and loving. Hannah's parents had been nice enough to co-sign on her other loans.

But she knew that they were uncomfortable with taking on more risk.

At least last year, she had a small part-time job. Of course, she had also had a rundown car that got her places. When that died, she was left with nothing for transportation. She'd had to take a bus just to get to campus. Maybe coming here had been a big mistake.

Amber left the building feeling despondent. She could always drop a couple of classes and save a bit of food money there, but that was just prolonging the problem. She simply had to get some income. She would move to a smaller apartment except that she was certain nothing cheaper existed. And the dorm fees were even more expensive because you had to buy the meal plan that came with it. As she dragged herself back to the apartment, Amber wondered if anyone would hire her full-time without a college degree.

Opening her door, Amber saw the empty breakfast plate and carried it to the sink. Sniffling, she washed up the few dishes before stretching out on the mattress. It sank disturbingly low. Just great! The mattress definitely leaked.

When the tears came, she let them flow, no longer caring. She thought of her mom, sitting in the trailer park getting drunk in the middle of the day. Was she destined to end up with a similar life? Maybe it was true that you couldn't escape your past. Huddling into a ball, Amber cried herself to sleep.

A few times, she heard her cell phone ring. She ignored it and burrowed deeper into her covers. The leaky mattress had lost most of its air and barely supported her body. Only when she couldn't persuade her bladder to wait any longer did she finally drag herself from the floor. Sticky with sweat, she stared at her reflection in the mirror. Her hair clung to her splotchy face.

Ugh! She looked as disgusting as she felt. Turning on the water, she stripped and stepped into the shower. Her stomach gurgled and she remembered she hadn't eaten since breakfast. She had no idea how late it was. She didn't really care.

As she lathered her hair, she started feeling lightheaded. No, not now! She needed to at least rinse all this shampoo out. Kneeling carefully, she squatted on her knees and let the shower do the work of rinsing. The first edges of black crept past her eyes. She reached up frantically to turn off the water. Her neck burned and she felt herself breaking into a cold sweat. Leaning back, she allowed her body to slide down the tub. She lay against the cold porcelain, trembling, fighting unconsciousness.

She was so stupid. She should have at least had some bread and jam. Now here she was stuck in the bottom of the bathtub, freezing. After several minutes, she tried to raise her head but was too dizzy. Then she thought to raise her legs and prop her feet against the faucet. Maybe the extra blood flow would help.

With a growing sense of panic, she realized that no one would know that she was here. Other than Hunter, she hadn't made any friends yet. Would he check up on her again? Maybe knock and simply go away when she didn't answer the door?

She had to get up! But her body refused to cooperate. Against her will, she passed out.

Chapter 5

When she woke again, it was to Hunter's anxious voice yelling for her.

"In here," she croaked, her voice weak.

There was no way he could hear her. She weakly reached up for the bottle of shampoo and flung it on the floor.

Oh, no! He couldn't find her naked. Using every bit of remaining strength, she leaned over and tugged the corner of the towel hanging next to the tub. She managed pull the material on top of her just as Hunter burst through the door.

"Hi," she whispered. "What's going on?"

"Again?" he asked incredulously. "Stay put and I'll be back in a second."

Amber giggled at that last part. It wasn't like she was going to leap out of the tub at any second.

Hunter came back a few minutes later. After placing a blanket on top of her towel, he scooped her up and carried her out of the bathroom. The deflated mattress was now folded up, topped with pillows and shoved against the wall. A plate with bread and jam rested on the makeshift crate table.

Hunter placed her on top of the pillows and then picked up each of her arms. After running his rough fingers over the interior of both arms, he sighed.

"Thank goodness!"

Amber thought it was a weird thing to say. But she was too busy fighting nausea and dizziness to really care.

"What are you doing? I need to eat," she mumbled.

As humiliating as it was, she had to let Hunter feed her tiny bites. When she could sit up without feeling faint, Hunter propped her against the wall.

"Later, we'll get some real food into you," he said gruffly. "But first we need to have a heart to heart chat."

Amber tried to shift away. Unfortunately, she couldn't wriggle around too much. Being naked beneath the blanket limited her options.

"Maybe I should get dressed first."

Hunter shook his head.

"And lose my advantage? I don't think so."

Amber frowned. "I could make you leave."

Hunter nodded thoughtfully. "Of course you could. But that would force me to make some phone calls. And that might lead to awkward questions from complete strangers."

"What are you talking about? What kind of phone calls?"

Had she made a mistake by letting Hunter in? Was he like one of those attractive killers like in the movies? Amber wondered how many steps it would take her to get to the door.

"Look, I'm saying all the wrong things. I'm obviously scaring you."

Hunter slid backwards to put more space between them.

"I'm sorry. I'll turn my back if you want to get dressed."

Amber pointed at a box in the corner of the room.

"I have clean clothes in there. Push it over her and then go sit in the corner of the kitchen."

To his credit, Hunter followed her directions immediately. He squeezed himself between the radiator and refrigerator.

"How's this?"

"Just stay there. I'll let you know when I'm done."

Amber put her clothes on beneath the blanket just to be on the safe side.

"Okay, you can come back," she said once dressed.

Hunter returned and pointed at a spot a few feet from where she sat.

"Is this okay?"

Amber nodded.

"Do you always threaten perfect strangers?"

She watched him wince.

"How many times does a person have to save you before they stop being a stranger?"

Ouch! Amber flushed. Maybe she had over reacted a little bit.

"You seem a little too involved in what is going on with me."

Hunter stared at her with those awesome green eyes. Then he dropped his head and played with his shoelaces.

"As a TA, I work for the school. That means that I have both a moral and legal obligation to report any student who might harm themselves. Intentionally or not."

Amber gaped at him.

"You think what? I'm on drugs? I'm trying to commit suicide?" she asked incredulously. "How dare you!"

Hunter remained calm. Was he trying to hide a smile?

"I think right now that you want to conk me in the head. Beyond that I don't know what to think. But I would like to help you with whatever it is that you're going through."

Amber couldn't help herself. After all she was arguing with the same person who had saved her. Twice. She grinned.

"I *will* conk you in the head if I feel it's necessary."

Hunter slid back several more inches. He wasn't smiling. He cupped his chin in his hands.

"That was supposed to be funny," she said, her voice contrite.

What if the school found out about her finances. Could they cancel her classes? Send her back to her mother?

Running a hand through his hair, Hunter sighed.

"Okay, Gorgeous, let me tell you what I think is going on and you tell me if I'm right."

Amber stared at him. *Gorgeous?* Was her low blood sugar affecting her hearing?

"First, I'm pretty sure you're not doing drugs. No marks on your arms and you don't fit the pattern."

Amber gaped at him. He had actually suspected drugs? What kind of person did he think she was?

Hunter must have guessed at what she was thinking.

"Don't take it the wrong way. I was a camp counselor in high school and freshman year of college."

He shrugged. "Rich. Poor. Jocks. Nerds. I've seen all types get hooked."

"You don't have the right to make assumptions!" Amber shouted at him, not even sure why she was so angry. Maybe because she wanted him to think she was better than she thought of herself.

Hunter drew back with a chuckle. "Wow. What a temper."

"Stop laughing at me!"

Hunter looked stung. He unfolded his legs and crawled closer to her.

"I would never make fun of you. I like you too much."

Amber drew back in disbelief.

"How can you say those things to me when you have a girlfriend?"

Now it was Hunter's turn to look surprised. He cocked his head to one side and a lock of hair fell alluringly over one eye.

"Wait. What? I don't have a girlfriend."

"Big chested Kayla!" Amber shouted. "Remember her and her ridiculous five inch cherry red nails?"

Hunter's eyes widened.

"Kayla? Are you serious?"

Amber studied Hunter's expression. Was he lying? Or had Kayla lied?

"Why would she tell me you were her boyfriend?"

Hunter rubbed a hand over his face. He pushed his hair away from his face.

"I don't know. But I've had zero interest in her. Or anyone else."

He paused and pondered her. He shook his head and the lock of hair fell back over one eye.

"At least until now."

Chapter 6

Amber tried to hide the smile sneaking onto her face. She didn't have to feel guilty about Kayla anymore.

But Hunter still looked serious. Oh. He was still expecting answers.

She swallowed hard. How could she tell him everything. Sure, he liked her now. But how would he feel when he found out about her uncaring, trailer trash mother? Or how broke she was? He was bound to lose interest.

"Okay, so I'm not on drugs or a criminal." She stared at the ceiling.

"I'm just broke. Dead broke. I can't afford this dinky apartment and I've been rationing my food for the past few weeks. I've tried to eat less so that I can buy books and paint supplies for class."

She felt her chin quiver. No! She would not cry now.

"I've always had an issue with low blood sugar. Sometimes I just wake up with it. It's worse when I don't eat right. I went to the infirmary once, but they didn't think it was a big deal. Just told me to try to have snacks around for when it happened."

Amber sneaked a look in Hunter's direction.

He lifted a finger and twirled it as though to indicate she should continue.

"What else? Oh, I have a horribly dysfunctional family. My father left when I was a baby and we never heard from him again. My mother is a raging alcoholic. Lives on welfare in a trailer park. She attracts loser boyfriends who always try to get their hands on me. She wanted me to stick around so she could get extra food stamps. I couldn't wait to leave. I'm never going back."

Amber felt the tears slipping down her cheeks. She thought she had deadened herself when it came to her parents. But beneath everything was the fear that she would one day turn out the same way. Maybe she was destined to never get ahead in life.

"My mother would rather me work some dead end job and give her money to buy booze than go to college."

Finally, it was too much, and she started to sob. "I don't need her."

Hunter got to his knees and crawled over.

"I'm so glad you told me, Amber. That's the kind of stuff you don't need to keep inside."

He stood up and went into the bathroom. When he returned, he had a handful of toilet paper.

She blew her nose and tried to get her emotions in check.

"Really, I'm fine," she said, sniffling. "It isn't like she suddenly became a bad parent. I've always been more responsible than she was. I think I was just a mistake to her and she resented me."

Hunter cupped her chin gently. "You are definitely not a mistake, Gorgeous. That's all we need to say about your family life right now."

Amber giggled. The combination of hunger, coming clean, and being called "gorgeous" was making her beyond delirious. She couldn't believe that Hunter wasn't totally repulsed by her past.

Hunter took a deep breath.

"Okay, this is what's going to happen. First, I'm ordering pizza from my favorite place. My treat. Then, you are staying at my apartment tonight."

Amber gaped at him. "At your apartment? I may be broke but I'm not that kind of girl!"

Now it was Hunter's turn to blush. His eyes widened.

"What? No! I didn't mean . . . That is . . . My roommate and I have a guestroom. With a separate bed and shower."

"Oh. Well, if that's the case."

Hunter's blush spread to Amber's face. Great! She had just accused her hero of wanting to sleep with her. Maybe he had called her "gorgeous" to make her feel better. It was probably part of some spiel he learned as a camp counselor to calm down anxious people. How awkward could this be?

"Tomorrow, we're going to figure out your financial issues."

Hunter had regained his casual demeanor and gestured at her books on the floor.

"What would you like to bring with you?"

Her toe was still bruised and painful when she carefully put on socks and sneakers. When she finished, she saw Hunter texting.

"All set?"

In the hallway, Hunter turned and scooped her up in his arms.

"I'm feeling fine," she protested halfheartedly, not wanting to admit that she enjoyed nestling in his arms. "You can't keep carrying me all the time."

Her conscience laughed.

Oh, please! You protest too much. Just admit that you are eating up all this attention.

Hunter ignored her. When he stepped outside, Amber saw a muscular guy with sandy hair holding open the door to a Range Rover.

"Amber, this is my roommate Caleb. Caleb, this is Amber."

"Hi, Amber, nice to meet you."

Caleb held out a hand. He had a friendly, easy-going smile.

Amber shook his hand shyly. She wondered what Hunter had told his roommate.

"Nice to meet you to, Caleb."

Hunter carefully put her in the back of the Range Rover and got in beside her.

"Safety first," he said as he helped buckle her in before harnessing himself in.

Caleb grinned back at them from the front.

"Nice to be driving for a change, Hunter."

"Don't get too used to it," Hunter muttered. "And drive the speed limit. I don't want a single scratch or dent on this."

Caleb laughed as he pulled out into the street.

They quickly passed the college campus and traveled toward the suburbs. The farther Caleb drove, the nicer the houses got. Finally, they arrived at a large Victorian with a wide, circular drive.

"The house has two apartments," Hunter explained. "Caleb and I have the top floor and a professor and his family live on the bottom."

Amber unbuckled her seat belt and tried to exit the car. But a bout of dizziness overcame her. Hunter caught her and grimaced.

"I should have gotten you something more substantial to eat earlier."

Caleb leaned over the front seat.

"Want me to heat up those leftover meatballs from lunch? That should hold her until the pizza gets here."

Hunter gave his roommate a grateful smile.

"Thanks, man. That would be great."

He turned to Amber. "Do you like meatballs?"

Amber gave a small smile. "Mm . . . Meatballs!"

Caleb hustled out of the car and jogged up the flight of stairs leading to the second floor.

Hooking his arms around her waist, Hunter eased Amber across the backseat and then easily lifted her in his arms.

"I suppose I should be grateful that you weigh so little."

He carried her up the steps and through the opened door.

Inside, Amber found herself in a spacious living room with a comfortable sofa and several chairs, all soft leather. Framed paintings covered the walls. The apartment was impeccably clean. It definitely did not resemble a typical student pad. Hunter and Caleb must be insanely wealthy to have this kind of place as students. And Hunter's Range Rover? She knew those were incredibly expensive.

Amber felt like she didn't belong. Her second hand clothes suddenly felt cheap instead of chic. She couldn't believe that she had just admitted to Hunter that she grew up in a trailer. But most of all she suddenly wondered if she was simply a pity case. A sympathy rescue.

Hunter deposited her on the sofa. "I'll get some drinks. Stay here."

The living room was open to a large, modern kitchen with beautifully stained dark cabinets, stainless steel appliances and granite counter tops. The microwave dinged. When Caleb opened the door, a delicious aroma spilled out. As if in answer, Amber's stomach emitted a deep gurgling grumble.

Caleb brought over the plate of meatballs on a wicker tray.

"I feel like I'm at a resort." Amber giggled nervously.

But her hunger quickly overshadowed her shyness and she bit into the first meatball.

Hunter returned with two glasses of soda.

As food entered her system, Amber's brain sprang back to life.

"Hey, how did you get into my apartment?"

Hunter frowned.

"You left the key in the door. I was terrified when I saw the door like that and you didn't answer right away."

Amber filled him in on her trip to the Financial Aid Office.

"So I guess I was just out of it when I came inside."

She got quiet a moment and then Hunter nudged her.

"No more thinking about anything but food and sleep tonight, okay? I promise that I'll help you figure it all out tomorrow."

An hour later, filled with pizza, Amber found herself nodding off as Caleb and Hunter talked about a new Art Exhibit at the Museum.

Hunter showed her a small bedroom with a dresser and neatly made bed.

"This is the guest room. Hardly gets used. Sheets are clean and so is the bathroom through that door. Plenty of soap, shampoo and fresh towels for in the morning."

Sitting on the edge of the bed, Amber slipped off her shoes and tugged off her socks. She felt as if she had stepped into a dream.

"Goodnight." Hunter closed the door behind him as he left the room.

After changing into pajamas, Amber crawled into the inviting bed. The sheets smelled like lavender. Within minutes she was asleep.

Chapter 7

Waking up the following morning, Amber rolled over with a happy sigh. For the first time in weeks, she starting the day with a sore back. She couldn't figure out how her bed had gotten so luxurious. And then she opened her eyes, jolting back to reality. Of course this wasn't her bed. This wasn't even her apartment.

She sat up quickly, blinking at the bright sun streaming through the window. The walls of the room were a soothing mint green. A few paintings of fruit and flowers hung on the walls. An old-fashioned wind up clock showed the time – a few minutes before seven. She wasn't sure when she had fallen asleep the night before. However, she felt completely rested. She climbed reluctantly out of bed and entered the small adjoining bathroom.

Though small, the bathroom was modern and impeccably clean. Apparently Caleb and Hunter were clean freaks, she thought with a smile. Either that or nobody ever used this bathroom. On the marble counter was a folded towel and washcloth. Peeking into the shower, she saw a small basket of assorted shampoo, soap and conditioner samples. On the back of the door hung a soft white robe.

She had just turned on the water and undressed when she heard a soft knock on the bedroom door. Turning off the water, she put on the fluffy robe and padded across plush carpet to answer it.

"Good Morning." Hunter greeted her with a giant smile. His hair was still wet from showering and there was a dab of shaving cream just below his ear.

"Good Morning! I have to thank you for the best sleep I've had in ages."

"Glad to hear that. Any plans on passing out in the shower this morning?"

Amber laughed. "Not unless you miss carrying me around."

Hunter smirked. "Oh, I miss carrying you around. But I'd rather you were fully conscious when I do it."

Amber flushed. "Well, um . . . Guess I better get ready so we aren't late for class."

Hunter grinned. "I'll just sit on the bed while you shower. Just to be on the safe side."

"Really, Hunter, I'm fine this morning!" Amber tried to push him out the door.

"I promise I won't peek!" Hunter held his hands up and moved back. "I just want to be where I can hear you if you start to feel faint."

Amber wanted to argue but she knew they didn't have time.

"Fine, but don't move one inch from that bed."

"Yes, ma'am!" Hunter theatrically sat on the bed and pretended to study a painting on the wall. He propped on finger on his chin and looked skyward.

Starting the water again, Amber opened a drawer and was surprised to find her toiletry bag inside. Although the previous night was a bit hazy, she was pretty sure she hadn't grabbed it. Hmm. Very weird.

"Can you make it a quick shower," Hunter called out. "I need to get to class early."

"Okay," Amber called out.

She opened her bag and found a hair band for a pony tail. She bathed and dried off. After brushing her teeth and applying a little lip gloss, she wrapped the fluffy robe around her and exited the bathroom. Hunter was gone.

On the bed was the box of clean clothes from her apartment. Had he gone over there this morning?

In the kitchen, she found Caleb drinking a cup of coffee and taking notes from a textbook. Hunter was on his cell phone in the far corner of the living room.

"Good morning. One of Hunter's models is sick and canceled for the day. He's trying to get somebody else to come in."

"Good morning."

Amber slid into a leather padded chair and reached for a platter of French toast and turkey bacon.

"Thanks for the hospitality last night. Just sorry I fell asleep so quickly."

"No problem," Caleb said. "It's good to see Hunter have something of a social life."

Amber glanced from Hunter to Caleb as she savored a sweet bite of French toast dipped in syrup. Did Caleb think she was Hunter's girlfriend?

"Wow, this French toast is awesome! Who made it?"

Caleb laughed. "I wish I could take the credit, but this is my Mom's creation. She spoils me. She makes up huge batches, freezes them, and brings them over from time to time."

"Pass on my regards to your mom."

Amber wolfed down several more pieces and following it up with a huge glass of juice.

"What about me? I microwaved the bacon."

Hunter, hanging his head as though his feelings had been hurt, walked into the kitchen to join the others.

"And you did a marvelous job!"

Amber held up a strip of the bacon. "See? This is my third piece."

Hunter's phone beeped and Caleb laughed.

"No need to worry about being late when you're around Hunter."

"Punctuality is a gift!"

He and Caleb began clearing away dishes.

A half hour later, Hunter dropped Caleb off at the far end of campus for his morning classes and then found a parking spot not far from Amber's apartment. He seemed distracted.

"Were you able to get a model for this morning?"

Amber lengthened her stride to keep up with Hunter's fast pace.

Hunter sighed. "Okay, I'm afraid that you're going to get angry. But the only model that was available this morning was," he paused a beat, "Kayla."

He cringed as he glanced over at Amber.

Amber considered for a moment.

"So you seriously never dated Kayla?"

Hunter shook his head emphatically.

"No. Never."

"So why is she so possessive over you?"

Hunter veered off the regular pathway to take a shortcut through the grass.

"Her parents know my parents. She's been trying to go out with me since high school. But she just isn't my type."

"So I guess I just have to be a professional and draw big chested Kayla."

Hunter laughed and put an arm around her shoulders.

"Now that's the kind of attitude I like to see!"

Amber's smile faded when Kayla stormed by looking as though she wanted to strangle somebody.

Hunter shrugged his shoulders as they entered the Fine Arts building.

"I don't expect her temperament to be especially sweet this morning."

This is going to be an interesting class, Amber thought as she followed Hunter into the empty classroom. While Hunter set up the modeling platform, she took her usual seat. She had time for some quick sketches before class started.

She only looked up when she heard Kayla's loud voice. She resisted the urge to raise her head, certain that Kayla was watching her every move. Lifting just her eyes, she saw Hunter pulling Kayla into the corridor.

Part of her wondered if Hunter was telling the truth. Then she scolded herself. If Hunter really was interested in Kayla, Amber had done nothing to prevent him.

Hunter and Kayla returned, along with a throng of more students.

"Professor Collins has a meeting this morning," Hunter called out. "Find an easel and make sure you have enough paper. The model will be doing several sets of ten minute poses. Remember the rules."

Amber found an easel at the far end of the podium, not wanting to be especially close to Kayla.

Kayla stepped up on the platform wearing a large button up shirt and long shirt. When she stepped out of both the entire class started murmuring. But underneath she wore a canary yellow swimsuit.

She glanced around the room and found Amber. Then she knelt on the floor and sat back on her haunches. Her hands were clenched in fists.

She locked eyes with Amber as though taunting her. Look at my body compared to yours, she seemed to be signaling. Why would Hunter want you when he could have this?

Okay, Amber thought. So you have a better body than me. I'll give you that.

She heard the others around her begin to sketch. But her own hands seemed frozen. Kayla's ferocious glare had actually cast a spell on her. She sat there, feeling ridiculous, until Hunter approached her easel.

He leaned down and whispered in her ear.

"Don't let her get to you."

His hand crossed her blank paper and picked up a piece of charcoal. He made a dot three-quarters of the way down the page.

"I would start here and draw her core."

He let his hand rest against her own for just a second longer than necessary.

Kayla's eyes widened and her body stiffened. She had certainly gotten the point.

Hunter moved away casually and assisted another student.

Amber blew out a breath of air and started sketching. She used dark, bold strokes to show the anger and tension in Kayla's body, capturing even the blackness of her eyes. The tension carried the drawing. When she finished, Amber realized that it was a good sketch. She smiled a little, wondering how Kayla would feel about inspiring some of her best work.

Kayla's next pose was lying prone on the floor, arms outstretched. Again, Hunter came by and casually brushed Amber's hand as he regarded her work. With each pose, Hunter found some reason to stop by Amber's easel.

As soon as her last pose was finished, Kayla hurriedly dressed and left.

Amber sat back, casting a critical eye at her drawings. One of the girls to her right, a redhead with sparkling blue eyes, motioned to her.

"What's the deal with that chick?" she whispered. "She looked like she wanted to poke your eyes out!"

Amber just grinned and shrugged. Then she reconsidered and stepped over to join the girl at the other easel.

"I'm Amber. Is this your first class with live models?"

"I'm Megan. And I had an anatomy class over the summer." She giggled. "Most of them chubby, middle-aged men."

Amber looked over Megan's drawings and felt her heart sink.

"This is my first class and your sketches are a million times better than mine."

"I'm sure that's an exaggeration."

Suddenly Megan poked Amber in the stomach.

"Hi, Hunter."

Amber turned quickly, her breath quickening. She thought of his hand brushing hers earlier. Not a coincidence, right? Or had it been? She searched Hunter's face, but he was busy examining Megan's sketches. He stopped on one and started talking about shadows and lighting.

Amber stepped casually back to her easel, ears burning. What was it about him? Boys, even good looking ones, rarely made her feel flustered.

After seeing how good Megan's drawings were, her own work suddenly seemed amateurish. How had she thought that she had done a good job?

"Ah, Miss Holloway. Let's see what we have today."

Hunter slowly shifted between her earlier drawings, nodding his head appreciatively.

Amber glanced up to see that she and Hunter were the only two people remaining in the room.

"These have a lot of potential. Especially this one where Kayla is trying to shoot laser beams from her eyes."

Hunter put the drawing aside, giving her a full smile.

Amber grinned, unable to resist his charm. He was probably just trying find something positive about her work, but she found she didn't care.

"Thanks."

"You're still having problems with proportion, though, so that's something to keep in mind as you're working. Sometimes it helps to block out the body in simple shapes first. We can practice that later."

Hunter picked up her homework sketchpad.

"Looks like you're already a little behind on your homework. We'll have to get you on a schedule."

Amber sat still for a moment. "What do you mean by that?"

She flinched as she realized how harsh her voice sounded.

Hunter froze and then smiled tightly.

"As the TA, my obligation is to make sure all the students in class are keeping up. You have a problem with that?"

Even with the smile, there was a slight warning in his voice.

"Oh, of course not," she murmured, fumbling as she put away her things for the day.

Oh! So he was just speaking as the TA. She had to keep his professional role in mind in class. When she looked up again, Hunter was at the other end of the room, straightening up the supply table.

"When's your next class?"

"Eleven o'clock," she said, sighing.

Wednesdays and Fridays she had English from eleven to one in the afternoon. She would have to jog to her history class following that course. Fortunately, the elderly instructor seemed oblivious to latecomers.

Checking the wall clock, she saw it was almost ten. She could walk back to the apartment for a jelly sandwich. Or she could grab a candy bar from the vending machine. One of those was bound to hold her until three o'clock.

And then she groaned as she remembered the rest of her schedule. She had an astronomy class from three to five on Wednesdays and Fridays as well. What had she been thinking when she registered for classes?

Hunter touched her shoulder and she jumped.

"Sorry," he said, holding up his hands. "Didn't mean to startle you. Why don't we come and sit over here. I cleared a space on the supply table. I brought my laptop with me today."

Amber followed him over reluctantly. Apparently, this was going to be the finance talk he had promised her the night before. But, really, what did she have to lose?

Hunter fixed her with those incredible green eyes. Eyes she wanted to swim in.

"I know this is very personal, but I can't help you unless I know just how bad your finances are. Would you be willing to share that with me?"

Amber licked her lips. What did she have to lose at this point except her self respect. She inhaled deeply and twisted her hands in her lap.

"I guess so."

Twenty minutes later, Hunter had created a spreadsheet with all her expenses, debts, and loan money.

"It's not as bad as I thought," he said, smiling reassuringly. "I mean, you definitely have a financial crisis. Fortunately, your only real debt is the student loans."

"I just need a job!" Amber wailed, miserably looking at the spreadsheet.

Hunter sat back and tapped his chin thoughtfully with a paintbrush. He seemed nervous.

"Okay, I have an idea, but I'm not sure what you're going to think about it."

Suddenly wary, Amber narrowed her eyes.

"Your rent and utilities are sucking up most of your resources, right?"

He sat back as though gauging her reaction.

"So you're suggesting a cardboard box?" she asked sarcastically. "A few glow sticks to read by?"

"Of course not!" Hunter snapped. Then he softened his voice.

"How about sharing the apartment with Caleb and me? In the guest room," he added quickly. "We never use it anyway."

Amber thought with longing of that cozy little room, the modern bath, and the luxurious furniture. The offer was tempting. But what about her interest in Hunter? Was it wise to consider moving into the same house as the guy you had a huge crush on?

"I doubt if I can get out of my lease," she said, trying to stall for time.

"Let me handle that!" Hunter said, a bit too eagerly. "I'd be happy to speak with Mr. Hanson."

Amber stared at him. "How do you know who my rent goes to?"

Hunter smiled easily. "It's on the copy of the check on your bank statement."

Oh, she hadn't noticed that before.

Hunter's cell phone beeped and he jerked to his feet.

"I'll be back in a few minutes. Stay put!"

Without further explanation he dashed out of the room, leaving the laptop on the table.

Amber laughed as she heard him running down the hallway. She had never seen anyone so infatuated with time. As she waited, she looked over the spreadsheet. Seeing the costs lined up like that was sobering.

She made an instant decision. She would drop some of her classes. That would give her time to pick up a part-time job. The bonus was that the money she saved could go toward her food, books, and art supplies. She was pretty sure she could keep the loan money as long as she was at least half time.

Just making that decision gave her peace. She sat back to wait for Hunter. Her eye caught a blinking icon at the bottom of the laptop screen.

She moved the cursor to switch pages. A small pop-up box on the bank page warned of a time out in sixty seconds. Hunter must have forgotten to sign out of her account. She frowned. Something about Hunter's assertion about her landlord bothered her.

She clicked the box to remain signed in and scrolled through the recent transactions. Although she had yet to make an actual rent payment, she had written a check for the deposit that summer.

After finding the debit from her account, she clicked on the check icon. A photocopy of the canceled check appeared on the screen. Hmm . . . That was weird. The Rental Management Company had signed the check. Now that she thought about it, she was sure she had not made the check out to him specifically.

How in the world had Hunter known the name? And why had he lied to her? Was this some kind of scam? Was he trying to play her? But why? It didn't make sense. But she wasn't letting him leave this room again until she got an answer.

Chapter 8

By the time Hunter returned, flushed and sweating around his temples, Amber had worked up a righteous anger. She coldly watched him place a paper sack on the table.

"I got you a small snack to take to class with you," he huffed. "I know you don't have time to get lunch this afternoon."

His grin faded as she scowled at him.

"What is it? What happened?"

Shaking with anger, Amber stood up and pointed to the laptop.

"I looked at the bank statement. I never put Mr. Hansom's name on the check."

She waited for his response.

"Just a second," Hunter panted.

He walked over to the sink, turned the water on, and stuck his entire head under the spray. He slowly rinsed his face, hair and neck. When he straightened, he shook his head like a wet dog. Finally, he stared at her, raised his tee-shirt, and calmly dried his face with the bottom of the shirt.

Amber involuntarily drew a breath at the glimpse of his taut, smooth stomach. He inched the shirt up higher to dab at the back of his neck with the fabric. Grinning, he dropped the shirt back down. He walked over, his blazing green eyes intense.

"You're so beautiful when you're angry," he whispered.

Amber blinked hard to clear her head. She found her tongue.

"How do you know about my landlord?"

Hunter ducked his head. A section of wet hair flopped onto his forehead. He shrugged apologetically.

"I have to confess that I did a little snooping."

Amber wanted to reach up and tuck Hunter's damp hair back in place. Instead, she punched him in the stomach.

"Why would you do something like that? Don't you know it's creepy?"

Hunter backed away, holding his midsection.

"Impressive jab," he huffed. "I'm sorry. But you didn't give me much choice. I should have just filed an incident report with Student Services. But I like you. I was trying to give you a break."

"I still don't understand why you would need to file a report!" Amber shouted. "All I did was get a little dizzy and faint. Stop using your titty bitty student job as a way to get your way with me!"

Hunter froze and his face darkened.

"Atty bitty student job?" His voice was cold. "Is that what you think?"

His eyes were like hard pebbles.

"I didn't mean . . ." she tried to say but Hunter cut her off.

"If you didn't have English class in a few minutes, I would . . ."

Amber cut him off. "I'm dropping that class later today."

She narrowed her eyes. "So why don't you show me exactly what you would do?"

Hunter looked startled and then grinned, stepping forward.

She backed away, but found herself sandwiched between him and the classroom whiteboard. She could have fought him, could have gotten away, but he hadn't even touched her.

Only those amazing green eyes pinned her there, helpless. She felt his body heat even through the damp tee-shirt. Water trickled down his neck.

Hunter raised both hands and supported himself against the whiteboard. "Say you'll be my roommate," he whispered, his breath sending shivers down her back.

"Please. No strings attached. I would never forgive myself if something bad happened to you."

Amber tried to think straight. She was swept up in the moment, his closeness making her head spin.

"It's too fast," she hedged. "I'll just be trading rent for my apartment for rent for your place. I don't see how that's helping."

"You don't have to pay anything," he said, like it was perfectly normal to ask a relative stranger to move into your house for free.

"You don't even really know me," she objected. "That's insane."

"It's what I want to do for you."

He sounded sincere but her past was what scared her the most. Wasn't this what her mother would have done? Let some guy take care of her. What was he expecting in return?

"I . . . just . . . can't," she said lamely. "I'll figure something out."

"You're so stubborn! It isn't a sign of weakness to let a fellow human being help you out."

"You have no idea of what I've had to fight for!" she screamed at him. "There was nobody . . ."

Hunter cut her off by shifting closer. Suddenly, all she was aware of was his body and the current of electricity buzzing between them. She told herself to move. But her body was ignoring any rational thought.

She opened her mouth to object. But no words came out. Hunter's beautiful green eyes hypnotized her.

All her anger had simply evaporated as he calmly stared at her. But as her anger cooled, her body began to warm. She suspected that she only had to shove him away and she would be released. But, suddenly, she wanted to be pinned to that whiteboard by his body. She wanted to get even closer. The charge between them made her body hum.

And then Hunter seemed to come to his own senses. He backed away, looking shaken.

"I don't want you to feel threatened into saying yes. I just want . . . to help," he finished lamely. "I've always had everything I needed."

"But why me?"

"Why not you? And once you get on your feet again, I'll even help you find a new place if you want."

He pleaded with his eyes. Those beautiful eyes.

Flustered, Amber tried to think of a plausible objection. But she was in a state of confusion.

"Okay, okay," she answered at last, trying to catch her breath, to return control to her thoughts.

Hunter moved a step forward and her pulse quickened.

"And you'll let me talk to your landlord?"

"What?" She forgot what they were talking about.

He pulled away a few inches. "The landlord?"

"Fine!" she yelped at last.

Hunter rewarded her with a wide smile. He looked like a little kid who just gotten free range in a toy store.

For a second she thought he might even kiss her. But then his phone beeped and ruined the moment.

She was tempted to smash it to bits.

Predictably, Hunter pulled away. At least he had the sense to look disappointed.

"I've got to get you home before my next class."

He gathering up his things, clasped her hand, and hurried out of the building.

"Can't you just be a little late?" she suggested, struggling to keep up with his long strides.

"Not my thing."

But he paused to slip his laptop bag over his shoulder before turning and swooping her off her feet.

"Hey! Put me down!"

Amber struggled in his arms, aware of all the snickers around her as Hunter shouldered his way through a throng of students.

"Bet I run even faster than you do," she blurted.

That did it. Amber's feet abruptly hit the ground as Hunter unceremoniously dropped her.

He didn't even wait before sprinting away.

"Hey! That's cheating!" She charged after him.

They were already halfway down the center, paved path near the main gated entrance when Amber sprinted off to the side to take the shortcut through the lawn. She was delighted to see the laptop whacking Hunter in the side. That should slow him down.

"Slow poke!," she taunted him.

Hunter paused and grinned. He slipped the laptop bag off his shoulder and tucked it under his arm like a football.

Amber, realizing he had been toying with her, fled across the lawn. Sure enough, Hunter passed her within half a minute and left her gasping after him. By the time she reached him, he was perched on the lawn and lazily chewing on a blade of grass.

"Show off!"

Hunter merely stood, grabbed her hand, and ran with her to the parked Range Rover.

Amber had to watch his smug smile the entire drive to his apartment. Correction. Their apartment. As much as she hated to admit it, she was glad to be staying there. She only hoped that Hunter could talk the landlord into letting her out of the lease. She still had her doubts.

"Don't forget your lunch," Hunter reminded her, setting the paper bag from earlier on the kitchen table.

"Thanks. But how am I getting to history class?"

Hunter grabbed a bag of pretzels from a cabinet and a bottle of water from the fridge.

"Caleb will take you. I leave the car near his class. He has an extra set of keys so he can come home for lunch before his one o'clock class."

With a small wave, Hunter bolted out the door.

Chapter 9

Amber sank into a seat at the table. She was keyed up both physically and mentally. Her stomach gurgled loudly to remind her how hungry she was. She pulled the paper sack closer and removed the contents, appraising the food appreciatively.

Thinking she was going to be eating in class, Hunter had gotten her all finger foods. There was a neat stack of pepperoni slices, several types of cubed cheese, crackers, a small bag of sliced apples, and a bottle of water.

Smiling, she popped a pepperoni slice into her mouth and chewed as she got out her History Syllabus. After missing yesterday, she knew she had to do a lot of reading to catch up. She was still taking notes when she heard a car pull up outside.

Peering out the living room window, she saw Caleb climbing out of the driver's seat of the Range Rover. She hurried back to the table, not wanting him to see her spying.

"Hey, Amber," Caleb called out as he entered the front door. He dropped his backpack on the sofa.

He didn't seem surprised to see her. Hunter must have texted him.

"Hi, Caleb, how was class?"

Caleb shrugged. "Okay, I guess. I can't wait to get out into the real world. Sitting through even a good class kills me."

"What's your major?" Amber asked as Caleb grabbed a soda, cold cuts, and bread from the fridge and sat across from her.

"Art, but I'm focusing on photography." Caleb assembled a massive ham and cheese sandwich.

"By the way, you can eat whatever you find in the fridge. We share everything."

"Thanks, I already had something."

Amber continued reading and taking notes from her History book while Caleb ate and checked messages on his phone.

Caleb's beeping phone startled her.

"Is that what I think it is?" she asked incredulously.

Caleb groaned. "Trust me. This isn't my idea."

He grinned. "You forget to pick your roommate up a few measly times and he commandeers your phone to program it with annoying alarms."

Amber laughed. "So how long did you forget him?"

Caleb grimaced. "Only twenty minutes the first time. But last spring I got caught up in a project and sort of stranded him for over an hour."

"Oh, I can't even imagine how mad he was!" Amber chuckled.

Caleb shook his head with a wry grin.

"Trust me. There was some flavorful language coming out of his mouth."

He stood up and stretched.

"Now he programs alarms for all my classes. My professors are all confused."

He grinned and grabbed his backpack.

"I used to drag in to class at the last minute. Now I arrive before the professors. It's messing with their minds."

Amber quickly gathered up her books.

"I guess I better get used to getting to class on time as well." She followed Caleb out the door.

Caleb was able to find a parking spot off campus. They walked toward class together before Amber headed to the right for her history class and Caleb continued straight toward the Science Building.

"Head for the fountain in front of the Student Union when class is over," he called out. "That's where I meet up with Hunter before we go home."

Not even the professor was in class when Amber walked into the room. Sighing, she got out her notes and continued reading. She also checked the attendance policy in her syllabus. Fortunately, the policy was lenient. Showing up was apparently optional, as she soon discovered when only about half the students eventually wandered into the room.

At some point, Amber realized the lecture came directly from the book. So she continued reading and taking notes at her own pace. By the end of class, her fingers were cramped and aching, but she had covered a good bit of material. As she gathered her materials, she was surprised to see Megan from art class.

"Hey, I didn't know you were taking this class," she said, smiling at the red-haired girl. Megan was the sort of cute, shy girl who often got overlooked.

Megan smiled back. "I just added it. I saw you taking notes like crazy so I was hoping I could borrow them and get caught up."

"You're welcome to copy what I have," Amber told her. "But I missed yesterday's class. To be honest, I'm just taking notes from the book now because the instructor seems to be going straight from that."

"Thanks, that's good to know." Megan swung her backpack over her shoulder.

"In that case, I guess I'll just follow the book as well."

Megan followed Amber out of the classroom.

"So, I've been dying to ask if there is anything between you and Hunter."

She reached up to tuck loose red locks of hair behind her ears.

"I'm not really sure," Amber replied, laughing. "He's definitely cute but claims not to date. Have you heard anything?"

Megan's face wrinkled up as she considered the question.

"The girls who get turned down try to pass him off as gay. I haven't heard of him dating anyone."

She shrugged. "Maybe it's self-preservation. Sadly, I know plenty of girls going here to try to find a husband. With his money, he's a target."

"Are you serious?" Amber gaped at her. "I mean he does have a nice apartment and a Range Rover."

Megan laughed. "Honestly? You've never heard of his family? The Webbs are fabulously wealthy and a big benefactor here. Hunter's grandparents gave money for the library when it was being built."

Megan paused to adjust her backpack.

"I get the impression Hunter doesn't care about the money so much. I think he's just hoping to concentrate on his art. He's quite talented."

Amber stopped, trying to get her bearings, when she saw the Science Building. Although she had studied the map several times, she still had to think about where she was going.

"Which way are you headed," Megan asked. "I have to go to the library."

Amber hesitated. She really wanted more of a scoop on Hunter. But she wasn't sure if either he or Caleb had more classes after this one. She didn't want to make either of them late.

"I'm headed for the Student Union," she said, reluctantly. "Guess I'll see you in class tomorrow."

As the two parted ways, Amber tried to match the little she knew about Hunter with the fact that he was supposedly super rich. What was up with the worn jeans and paint-splattered tee-shirts? Was that his way to try to hide his wealth? Or did he simply not care about things like that?

As she walked along, she felt as though a stone was growing in her stomach. What if Hunter thought that she was after his money? Here she was, completely broke, and now he was giving her a place to live. What if he later thought it was all a ploy on her part?

"Hey, Amber, where are you going?" Hunter shouted.

Looking up, Amber realized that she had passed the fountain. She turned back, giving him a small wave. Caleb was about twenty feet away and held a Frisbee. While she walked back, they threw it back and forth.

"Is something wrong?" Hunter asked as the three of them walked back toward the car.

"Too much history jammed into my brain," she said, smiling and shaking off her anxiety.

When they reached the grass lawn at the front of the campus, Caleb jogged off to one side.

"Let's play a little Frisbee before we go back. I have a ton of homework and I need to clear my head."

Hunter looked at Amber. "Are you game?"

"Are you sure you can compete with me?"

Amber stretched her arms and did a couple of deep knee squats to limber up.

"Only one way to find out," Hunter said, grinning.

For the next half hour, they ran around like little kids, laughing when some of Hunter's throws overshot their heads. Amber tossed the Frisbee into the shrubs twice and grumbled as she got scratched up trying to retrieve it. But it wasn't until she accidentally pitched the Frisbee into the street, and the guys had to hold up traffic both ways so she could get it back, that they decided to quit for the day.

Out of breath and still laughing, they all piled into the Range Rover.

"Hey, we have a coupon for Chinese takeout," Hunter said, rummaging in the glove compartment. "Are you guys interested?"

"You know you don't even have to ask me," Caleb said. "I don't turn down food."

"Sounds good to me," Amber said.

The Financial Aid Office had given her a debit card with the remaining loan money. She would have to see about getting some groceries, though, rather than eating out so much. Whether Hunter accepted the money or not, she was certainly going to offer to pay for her share of dinner.

She was surprised that Hunter would use a coupon if he was so wealthy. Part of the act? Or was Megan wrong and Hunter was just an ordinary college guy. She couldn't just go up to him and ask if he was worth gobs of money could she? Hmm . . . A better way might be to simply Google him later.

After they got home, Caleb grabbed a drink and an apple from the fridge and headed to his room to study.

"I'll be in the cave until dinner time," he said, disappearing around a corner.

"The cave?" Amber asked, raising her eyebrows.

Hunter laughed. "That's the name I gave his room. He has the blinds drawn all the time so it's dark and gloomy in there."

He grabbed a couple of drinks from the fridge.

"Want to see my room?"

Amber followed him into a large, comfortable, bright room with an adjoining bathroom off to the side.

"Do all the rooms have their own private bath?"

This place must be even more expensive than she thought. Again, all her anxieties about money and being dependent on someone else surfaced.

"Yep. A good thing, too, so you don't have to share with us guys."

He sounded both flip and defiant. He flung himself backwards on the bed.

"My parents bought this house when I started college here. After I'm gone, they'll rent this part just like they rent out the bottom."

"Wow, that's really generous of them," Amber said, at a loss for words. "You know, I can still chip in, right? I don't want to take advantage of you."

Hunter turned his face to her, his eyes shining.

"You really mean that, don't you?"

"Of course I do!" Amber snapped. "Just because I . . ." she tried to say but was stopped when Hunter leaped off the bed and held up his hand.

"That's what I like about you," he said, stopping her with just one glance. "You're not trying to get anything from me."

He smiled sadly. "I don't meet a lot of people like that."

Suddenly he paused, looking curious.

"Did you know about me already?"

Amber was honest. "I had no idea about your family's money until today. Somebody in one of my classes mentioned it."

"Oh, I'm sure they did," Hunter said, his face hardening.

"No, it wasn't like that," Amber said, aware she had just inadvertently hurt him.

"She said you were a great guy and that she thought you were right about some girls . . ."

Hunter's eyebrows shot up.

"Look, she told me what a great guy you are. Let's leave it at that."

"So, you'll really stay here then?" he asked shyly.

"Yes, I'll stay. I'd have to be an idiot to want to go back to my apartment after sleeping in that luxurious bed."

"What? You don't want me to repair the camping mattress?"

"Only if you are planning some actual camping trips."

Amber laughed. "My back was taking a beating on that thing."

She explored the room. The white walls were bare with the exception of large sketches that had been tacked up with push pins. A plain bed with a simple comforter was pushed against one wall. The rest of the room, dotted with several easels, was obviously being used as an art studio.

Twisting, she noticed a small wooden plaque above a plain dresser against the wall. She went closer for a look.

The engraving was a quote that read: "Though a living cannot be made from art, art makes life worth living. It makes starving, living." – John Sloan, *John Sloan on Drawing and Painting.*

Hunter came up behind her and put his hand on her shoulders.

"I've always liked that quote. I suppose that must sound weird coming from a rich kid. But I guess it fits how I feel about where I come from. I don't care about making gobs of money. I just want to be an artist. I think I would do it even if I didn't have my parents helping me out."

Amber turned to smile at him.

"I have to say that I feel like that, too. Well, except for the rich parent part!"

She ran her fingers along the engraved words.

"But drawing does take me somewhere else when life gets crazy. And, yeah, it can make you forget you're hungry for a little while."

Hunter turned her around and looked at her grimly.

"But no more going hungry, okay?"

"Okay," said Amber. She paused a beat. "I guess I should get settled into my room."

Hunter gave a nod of his head, trying to unsuccessfully hide a smirk.

"What?" Amber asked.

"Nothing," said Hunter.

Amber passed through the living room and into the guest room – now her room. She wondered what Hunter was up to. She scanned the room for her suitcase, but didn't see it. She opened the closet door and stood there stunned.

Chapter 10

Hunter entered Amber's room. "I didn't know where you wanted everything so I'd be happy to move ..."

Amber turned and punched his gut for the second time that day.

His eyes widened, but he stopped talking.

"Did you skip class to do this?" she asked, daring him to lie to her.

"No," he said, shaking his head adamantly. "I don't skip class."

"I didn't think so." She stared at him. "So, when exactly did I become a foregone conclusion?"

"What?" He had the nerve to look confused.

"I don't remember agreeing to stay here until this morning after art class. So I'm kind of confused as to when you had time to bring my stuff over."

Amber watched Hunter squirm.

"So I just want to know, for the record, when exactly you did your good deed."

"Good deed?" Anger replaced Hunter's guilty look.

"Yes, I moved your stuff out last night while you were asleep. Because, frankly, I didn't see how in the world you could stay there without any money to pay your rent. And, further, yes, I did talk to your landlord. He was quite irate. Said you were already late with last month's rent. He already had eviction papers drawn up."

By this time Hunter was seething. His hands were clenched and the veins in his neck were bulging.

"Excuse me for being a decent human being and helping out someone who I thought was a friend."

"I'm not a charity case!" Amber screamed at him. "I would have paid the rent. I had enough to make it through this month."

She knew she was being crazy. But all she could think about was his help being like welfare.

"But what about the month after that? Can't you see how much trouble you're in? You passed out from sheer hunger twice! What would you have done if I hadn't shown up in your apartment yesterday?"

Hunter gestured at her things in the room with a shaking hand.

"So I guess I'm a total jerk for trying to give you something positive in your life for a change."

Chest heaving, he turned and stormed from the room.

"I can't deal with you right now."

Moments later, Amber heard the door slam and feet pounding down the stairs. She ran to the living room. Peeking out the large bay window, she watched Hunter jog down the driveway.

She was still so angry herself. She wanted to punish him for simply leaving in the middle of a fight. She struggled with the window and finally heaved it open. Pressing her head against the screen, she shouted at his retreating figure.

"This isn't finished, Hunter Webb!"

If he heard her, he didn't show it.

Once she couldn't see him, all the anger drained out of her. She felt exhausted and numb. She frankly didn't know what to think anymore.

"Is it safe for me to come out?"

Turning, Amber saw Caleb peering out of his room.

She nodded numbly. "I'm sorry. You shouldn't have had to hear all of that."

Caleb entered the kitchen, tossed his soda can in the recycling container, and pulled another drink from the fridge.

"One for you?"

Amber nodded, embarrassed.

Caleb sat down and tapped his hands nervously on the table.

"So, I wasn't trying to eavesdrop, but it was hard not to hear what you guys were screaming at each other."

"I just don't get how he did everything without asking me first. Who does something like that? I mean, I know he has the money. But he just met me."

Caleb sat silently for a few moments. Then he looked up earnestly.

"Look. Maybe it isn't my place to tell you stuff. But you should understand something about Hunter."

"I hope you aren't going to make excuses for him."

Amber sat down across from him and popped her soda open.

Caleb shook his head.

"He should have told you about bringing your stuff over. I get that. But you have to understand that, with the exception of our moms and the cleaning lady, you are the first girl he ever brought into this apartment."

He paused and waited for that to sink in.

"You have a cleaning lady?" Amber asked, incredulous. "What college student has a cleaning lady?"

Caleb slapped his forehead.

"Focus, Amber. We're talking about you being the first female Hunter Webb has ever brought to this apartment."

The nugget of information worked itself into her brain. Her mouth dropped.

"But he's a junior, right? You mean he's never had a girlfriend here?"

"Girlfriend? Are you kidding me? I'm talking about any girl."

Amber bit her lip. "Are you sure he isn't . . . um . . ."

She couldn't finish the thought.

"Gay?" Caleb grinned.

"No, I can assure you that he is not gay. In high school, he dated quite a bit. But sooner or later the girls always seemed to be more interested in his money than him."

Caleb shrugged.

"So when we came to college, Hunter vowed he wouldn't date anyone. He fills his time with his art and the TA job. The job has been great for him. He works hard and genuinely likes helping people."

Amber cringed, remembering her comment about his "itsy bitsy student job." No wonder he had been so hurt. She had attacked his one source of pride.

"But I have nothing!" she moaned, putting her head on the table. "I don't want him to ever think that I'm after his money."

Caleb put a hand on her shoulder.

"Look, Amber, I grew up knowing Hunter since we were little. I was the dorky kid from the wrong side of the tracks. He was the rich kid. But he never thought of himself that way. He has always been there for me. He even beat up a few kids in middle school who tried to trash my name."

Amber looked up with shame.

"Caleb, I'm so sorry. I just assumed that you were rich like him."

Caleb laughed suddenly. "I'm rich with good looks and intelligence. Or at least that's what I tell the ladies."

Amber grinned. "So, it's none of my business but . . ."

Caleb smiled. "It's okay. It was hard for me to accept living here for free and having his parents help pay for my tuition. But what helped was when his mom told me how much Hunter needed to have real friends who supported him."

Amber swallowed hard at that. Hunter had said that he thought that she was a real friend. She had no idea just how much that meant to him. She realized with a pang that she had judged him just as much as some people had judged her in the past. While he had kindly ignored her past, she had shoved his face in his.

Caleb took a drink and then played with the can.

"His mom helped me see that even with all his money, Hunter has gaps in his life. He has always had to wonder if people he meets see him as anything but dollar signs."

"I've royally messed up," Amber moaned.

"Hey, don't let him totally off the hook," Caleb warned. "You have a right to be mad at him. I just don't want you to leave."

He reached over and squeezed her hand.

"I think he really likes you. Even with all his ranting and raving, this is the first time in such a long time that I've seen him genuinely excited about a girl."

Suddenly, Amber heard footsteps coming up the steps.

Caleb bolted from the table.

"I was never here!" he whispered dramatically and disappeared into his room.

Amber tossed Caleb's empty soda can in the recycling bin and grabbed her backpack. She was lifting out her sketchbook when Hunter entered, breathing heavily and dripping sweat.

"I'm sorry I lost my temper like that," he said softly, standing still by the door.

"Me too," Amber said. "Maybe we should talk after you get a shower."

She smiled. "I can smell you from over here."

"What? You don't like a hot, steamy man?"

He smiled cautiously as he removed his sneakers and padded toward his room in stocking feet.

Amber placed her sketchbook on the table. With all the commotion, she needed to calm her nerves. She remembered that she was way behind with her homework sketches. Grabbing a charcoal pencil, she started sketching her hand.

A few minutes later, she heard the water going through the pipes as Hunter took his shower.

Caleb must have heard the pipes as well because he peeked out of his room.

"Everything okay?"

"I think so," Amber said. "We're going to talk when he finishes showering."

"Well, I'm getting hungry so I'm ordering dinner now."

He grinned. "Just in case you two start another war. At least I'll have food rations while I'm hiding out in my room."

Amber laughed. "I'm not planning on any more yelling today. I think you'll survive."

"Safety first," Caleb said with a chuckle, picking up his cell phone to place the order.

He handed her the takeout menu. "Let me know what you want. Hunter gets the same dish every time."

When Hunter came out, freshly showered and dressed in simple jeans and tee-shirt, Amber didn't know how to act. She sniffed the air theatrically.

"Ah, now that's an improvement!"

Hunter came over and ducked his head like a penitent little boy.

"I was afraid you would be gone when I got back."

Amber gently lifted his head. And nearly drowned in those beautiful green eyes.

"I'm sorry I reacted like a lunatic."

Hunter smiled. "You're a gorgeous lunatic."

Suddenly, Hunter's cell phone beeped.

"What now?" Amber asked, exasperated.

Hunter swiped the screen to turn off the alarm.

"Just a reminder to order dinner."

"Caleb ordered a little while ago while you were showering. He said you always eat the same thing."

"One day I might surprise him," Hunter said, as they stared at each other.

"Doubtful," Caleb said, causing both Amber and Hunter to jump.

"Also, per your rules, Hunter, there shall be no making out in common areas of the house."

He grinned. "And that's a direct quote from lover boy there."

Amber blushed but Hunter simply laughed.

"We weren't making out."

"Yet," countered Caleb. "But I'm going to be nice at this momentous occasion and take your Range Rover and go see a movie. Right after we eat, that is. If you two can keep your hands to yourself that long."

"A date?" Hunter asked. "The girl from the other night? Or is there a new girl in your life?"

Caleb clutched his chest theatrically.

"Careful, Hunter, I don't want Amber to get the wrong image of me. Besides, I can't help it if the ladies find me irresistible."

Hunter simply laughed and tossed Caleb the keys.

True to his word, Caleb left as soon as the Chinese takeout had arrived and all three had eaten. As soon as he was gone, Hunter was all business.

"How much homework have you done for Art Class?"

"Homework? Now?" Amber was incredulous.

"I'm serious, Amber. Ben checks homework on Thursdays. He's fanatic about it being completed on time."

"Then I'm in trouble," Amber sighed. "Because all I've managed so far are some sketches of my hand."

"Then let's get going," Hunter announced cheerfully. "I'll be your model."

Chapter 11

Amber followed Hunter into his room with a pounding heart. Surely he was just going to be posing with his clothes on. So why was she sweating and blushing?

Hunter's bare feet padded across the dark wooden floor. For the first time, Amber noticed paint flecks spattered across the broad wood planks. Well, that explained the lack of carpet in his room.

Hunter stopped in front of an easel and clipped on a blank sheet of drawing paper. From a nearby workbench she hadn't noticed before, he opened a drawer and pulled out a box of charcoal pencils. He walked over to a closet and pulled out a large skeleton that hung from a pole.

"Mr. Bones? From class?" Amber giggled.

"What? Oh, no. This is his cousin, Bob," Hunter said, trying to frown but not quite succeeding.

"I can't believe you would mix them up. You've probably hurt his feelings."

"My apologies, Bob," Amber said, trying to keep a straight face. "You're much more handsome than Mr. Bones."

Hunter unhooked Bob from the pole and placed him on the floor.

Amber watched, amused, as Hunter pulled over some cushions and small boxes and began to drape Bob over them. When he finished, Bob was posing like any other model with two knees sticking up, his skull tilted to the side and arms flung behind his head.

Hunter stepped back, eyed his work, and then approached Bob to make some minor adjustments. When he was finished, he looked back at Amber and winked.

"Bob and I have a special relationship," he said, grinning.

"I see that," Amber said. "I certainly hope Bob isn't jealous of me," she added cheekily.

Hunter paused and his eyes twinkled.

"Bob's been wanting to get out into the world. Meet new people. Form new attachments."

"Sometimes moving out of your comfort zone is a good thing," Amber said, aware that he was talking about himself.

Hunter switched quickly to TA mode.

"I want to have a little lesson on proportions. With Bob's generous assistance, of course. Watch as I use simple shapes to get started."

As he spoke, Hunter quickly sketched a series of triangles, circles, and rectangles on the page.

Amber watched carefully as he held up his pencil at several intervals before making small marks and adjustments on the page. After that, he drew thicker lines to make the shapes flow together into the human form. From just the skeleton, he had imagined a completed human form. Finally, he removed his own drawing. He helped Amber clip her own sketchbook into place and then rummaged in the workbench for a timer.

"I want you to sketch for ten minutes."

Mimicking Hunter's instructions, Amber concentrated on getting shapes drawn in appropriate proportions. A couple of times, Hunter stepped up with a comment or suggestion. For the most part, however, he allowed her to work in silence.

When he called time, Hunter had her switch easels so that she could work from another angle. Finally, he called time again.

"Much better," he said with approval. "You learn quickly."

"Thanks," Amber said shyly. "You're a great teacher.

She paused, feeling embarrassed.

"I've been meaning to apologize for what I said about your job," she added hesitantly.

"I was just angry. I certainly didn't mean anything by it."

"Apology accepted," Hunter said gruffly.

He walked over to Bob and dragged the skeleton back to the closet.

"Bob's a good model. But he can be a little stiff."

Hunter pulled a stool to the center of the room and sat.

"See what you can do with my form."

Amber drew an inverted triangle to capture Hunter's wide shoulders and narrow hips. After a few seconds, she felt herself relax as she focused on his body as a simple form. She sketched as quickly as possible, not letting herself get bogged down in details. She pulled the easel around the room to capture his body from as many angles as possible.

By the time Hunter switched to his next pose, she was in full professional artist mode. When finished, Amber found that she was physically tired, with her hands and arms covered with charcoal smudges.

She stepped back to inspect her work. She thought she had done a good job. But she was anxious to see what Hunter thought.

He contemplated each page with a studious face.

"Greatly improved."

"Blocking out the shapes is brilliant. We talked about that in one of my classes last year, but I never got a chance to practice."

"I'm glad you agreed to be a roommate."

Hunter stared at her. His cheeks were flushed.

Is he going to kiss me? Should I say something?

"It's getting late. Maybe we should say goodnight."

Amber could have slapped herself. He was going to think she was rejecting him.

"Yes, I want to say goodnight."

Hunter approached until there was almost no space between them.

Amber could feel the heat of his body. She wanted to close the gap. To have him hold her.

Hunter's head tilted down.

Amber could hardly breathe. Up close she saw that those emerald eyes had tiny flecks of blue. She could smell Hunter's aftershave. Time slowed.

His lips found hers and his kiss was soft and sweet.

"Was that okay? I should have asked first."

"Of course," Amber stammered.

She surprised herself by reaching up, tugging his head down and kissing him back.

"Thanks again for the help."

Hunter stroked her cheek with his calloused fingers.

"I've wanted to do that since the day I met you."

He lifted her chin and kissed her again. He took his time, cupping her head in his hands and twirling his fingers through her hair.

Amber's knees trembled. This only happens in books!

"Good night and sweet dreams," Hunter finally murmured, breaking away.

Amber stumbled out of the room, down the hall and into her own room.

She stared at the ceiling for half the night with the memory of his lips on hers. And when she closed her eyes that night, she dreamed of those lovely green eyes.

Chapter 12

After the previous night's instruction from Hunter, drawing the live model in class seemed much easier. Using the shapes for her proportions was having a positive affect on her sketches. After class, Professor Collins praised her for her rapid improvement.

Hunter had been correct about homework as well. Several students groaned when informed that points would be taken off for missing sketches. Thanks to Hunter, Amber passed the first inspection.

After class, she stopped in the restroom to wash the charcoal off her hands. She was just drying her hands when Kayla walked, arms crossed against her chest.

"Hi, Kayla," Amber announced brightly, avoiding the girl's murderous eyes.

Kayla jerked a bright red talon in Amber's direction. Her voice shook with fury.

"I thought I told you to keep your hands off of Hunter," she snarled.

Amber swiveled around, assessing Kayla's mood.

"I had an interesting chat with Hunter. Seems that he is under the impression that he and you are not dating. Further, that he has never had any interest in you."

Kayla swiveled her head around to make sure that they were alone.

"You don't know who you're messing with," she threatened.

Amber laughed. "That's the thing. Maybe I do."

She calmly tossed her wet paper towels in the trash. She began to walk toward the door with her head held high.

"You're just some stray dog that Hunter feels needs attention," Kayla said. "He would never date some loser like you."

Amber stopped and clenched her fists. But she kept her temper and forced herself to sound casual.

"Then why are you so angry? Worried that a stray will steal is heart?"

Kayla's face turned white. She shoved past Amber and bolted from the room.

Following the girl out, Amber nearly collided with Megan.

"Are you okay?" her red-haired friend asked, her face concerned. "Kayla looks livid."

"Yes, are you okay?"

Hunter was suddenly by her side, angry. "If she messed with you . . ."

Amber held up a hand to cut him off.

"Relax. I'm fine. I think she finally gets the picture."

Hunter relaxed, wrapping an arm around her.

Amber peeked over his shoulder to give Megan a smile.

"See you in history class, Megan?"

Megan giggled and held two thumbs up.

Amber and Hunter walked out of the building arm-in-arm. For the first time in her life, Amber felt positive and happy about where things were headed.

Could her happiness last?

Chapter 13

Amber Holloway scraped the last of the vegetable fried rice out of the takeout container and mixed it in with the last few bites of her sweet and sour chicken. If she kept eating like this every night, she was going to have to purchase new jeans or start working out more often.

"Which one do you want?" Hunter held out two fortune cookies. "Choose well for your fate."

"How about I open both and pick the fortune I like best?" Hunter grinned.

"Ha! Nice try, but the cookie fairy doesn't work like that."

"Cookie fairy?" Amber teased.

She reached out and tapped his forehead with her finger. "I think your imagination is working overtime in there."

Hunter shook his head, making a lock of hair fall over half his face. He feigned a serious face.

"Only facts operate in this head. My mind is like a steel trap."

"Oh your mind is a trap all right," Amber said with a giggle.

She grabbed one of the pale, crispy sweets. After snapping the cookie in half and letting the sweetness melt on her tongue, she squinted at the small slip of paper.

"Hey, this one is kind of cool," Hunter said, reading from his fortune.

"A ship in harbor is safe, but that's not why ships are built."

"How about mine?" Amber asked. "If you want the rainbow, you have to tolerate the rain."

"Oh, that's a good one too!"

Hunter sprang from his seat, nearly knocking over his bottled water. He pinned both the fortunes on the small refrigerator clipboard they kept for messages.

Her belly stuffed, Amber got up and started clearing the table. She loved how Hunter pitched right in, rinsing the plates and stacking them neatly in the dishwasher.

"I've got to catch up on some reading for my history class," Amber said, reluctant to have dinner over with.

She would have much rather snuggled on the sofa with Hunter than work on homework. But they had agreed that they wouldn't let their budding relationship get in the way of school or grades.

Sitting at the cleared table, she opened her textbook and grabbed her notebook and highlighters. But her eyes kept darting to Hunter. From her vantage point, she could feast her eyes on Hunter's dark tussled hair and those amazing full lips. His tee-shirt was fitted and clung nicely to his frame.

Only the month before, Amber had been broke and starving in a tiny apartment she couldn't afford. Fast forward three weeks and here she was, living in this beautiful apartment with an incredibly handsome boyfriend and his lifelong best friend. Oh, and Hunter also happened to be insanely wealthy.

Not that the money mattered to her. She hadn't even known of his wealth when they met. In spite of Hunter's generosity with free rent, Amber had quickly gotten a job as a grocery cashier. Although not glamorous, the paycheck allowed her to pitch in for food. The only thing that made her feel better was that Caleb also lived there rent free.

Was this odd? Absolutely. Was she spending any time dwelling on it? For the moment, no. To be honest, she couldn't have even dreamed of a better scenario the previous year when she first decided to leave her unhappy home and transfer to Higgins College. Sometimes she was afraid she was going to wake up and realize it had all been a nice dream.

"Junk, junk, bill, junk, bill," Hunter muttered, sorting a giant pile of mail that had accumulated in a wicker basket by the door.

Amber watched him, grinning. She knew he probably wasn't even aware he was speaking out loud. It was one of his cute habits. As Amber watched him, feeling content, she noticed his torso stiffen. She sat straighter herself, her own body taut.

Hunter took a deep breath as he held up a small airmail envelope, festooned with foreign stamps. And in that instant, though it was inexplicable, Amber got a feeling of dread. She shoved the textbook to the side and sat next to Hunter on the sofa.

"What is it? Is something wrong?"

For several moments Hunter didn't say anything.

"It might be nothing," he said at last, grimacing. "Probably just a rejection letter."

"A rejection letter?" Amber felt chilled.

Hunter gave a short laugh.

"Okay, this sounds a little nuts. But a few months ago I applied for an internship in France. I figured it was one of those one in a million shots. But my mom insisted that I apply."

Amber swallowed hard. "Wow, an internship. Sounds exciting!"

She wondered if Hunter could tell that her cheerfulness was forced. She peered at the thin envelope, feeling nauseous. As Hunter took a deep breath and bit his lower lip, Amber saw how sharp his desire was. She clearly could not compete with an internship in another country.

Hunter slowly slid open the envelope and a slip of wafer thin stationery, along with a waft of perfume, slid out. The bulk of the letter was typed. But Amber spotted a small bit of elegantly written script at the end.

Amber watched Hunter's face. When his smiled widened, she felt torn between wanting his happiness versus her own selfish desire to keep him here with her. It was wonderful seeing him look so happy. But what would happen to her if he left?

"Good news?" She willed herself to smile.

"I got it, Gorgeous! I got it!" Hunter stood and pumped his fists in the air.

"I can't believe it! They accepted me!" Hunter's voice was filled with pride and wonder.

"She says that it took longer than they expected because they had more than a thousand candidates this year."

Amber fought to control her dismay.

"Wow. That's incredible that you got chosen from all of those other people."

A girlfriend was supposed to be happy. A girlfriend was supposed to be supportive. So why did she hope that this letter was all a big mistake?

Hunter collapsed back on the sofa. He took the letter, smoothed it out, and read it again.

"I was one of the few candidates from the US that speaks fluent French. They're trying to attract more Americans to their gallery."

Amber's mouth flopped open. "You speak fluent French?"

Hunter looked up for a moment as though trying to pay attention to her.

"Yeah, I'm actually a dual citizen. My mom is from Paris. She met my Dad in graduate school. We moved here when I was a little kid because Dad was starting a new division of the company."

He smiled and his face looked soft and happy.

"While my grandparents were alive, I spent most of my summers there."

"Wow. Oh, wow."

Amber suddenly felt very uncultured. She had barely passed her high school Spanish classes.

"So . . . How long is the internship?"

"Twelve weeks," Hunter said, his face radiant. "This is going to be so awesome!"

Twelve weeks? Okay, she could live with twelve weeks. Couldn't she? Amber licked her lips and tried to look enthusiastic.

"Oh, Amber, I'm such an idiot!"

Hunter bolted upright and scooted across the sofa.

"I wasn't thinking at all about how this makes you feel."

He pulled her close and gave her a long kiss.

"You'll still be my girl, right?" Hunter peered at her anxiously. "I know twelve weeks must seem like forever. But I'll rush right back to you."

Amber had to blink back tears of relief. He really did care.

"Hey, I'll have time to earn enough money to take you to a fancy restaurant when you get back," she said, trying to keep a smile plastered on her face.

"And you'll have to wear a suit and tie."

Hunter sighed, clearly relieved. He kissed her again and then hopped up from the sofa.

"I should really call my mom. Do you mind? I'll call from my bedroom so I don't disturb you."

"Of course not!" Amber lips felt frozen in place.

As she watched Hunter pad into his room, she realized that she didn't even know when he was leaving. She started to get up and follow.

But then she saw the letter, the object of all her sudden distress, lying on the coffee table.

Leave it! If he wanted you to read it he would have asked.

Sometimes her conscience was just a pain. Amber sat down at the table and attempted to read her assignment. But after reading the same page twice and not knowing what was going on, she sighed and pushed the book away for the second time that night.

She walked down the hallway and heard Hunter's voice. She didn't mean to eavesdrop but she found herself lingering just outside his door. But then she realized that she had no idea what he was saying.

He must be practicing his French while on the phone with his mom. Feeling guilty, Amber went back to the table and attempted her assignment for the third time. This time she made herself highlight two pages of text before she glanced over at the letter. Why couldn't she ignore the stupid thing?

Without thinking, she walked over and picked it up. The paper was strangely thin compared to American stationary. And the perfume wafting from it smelled exotic. Expensive. She glanced at the hallway, half expecting to see Hunter returning. She didn't want to look like she was spying. But she was going crazy not knowing all the details.

The woman's name was monogrammed on the stationary. Isabelle Lebas. Why did it have to sound like an attractive woman? Was this the woman Hunter would be working for?

An image popped into Amber's head of a sleek French woman busy sketching Hunter. Alone in a studio.

Stop it! You're being ridiculous. Hasn't Hunter given you every reason to trust him? Especially when he trusts so few people?

Hunter was a great boyfriend. He was always thinking of her needs. If anything, he was a little too controlling. But he had never made her feel anything but special.

True, they had never gone beyond kissing. Both of them agreed that they had to put limits on the relationship in order to remain roommates. But still. How could she compete with some sophisticated woman in Paris? For the first time ever, Amber felt jealous.

She turned her attention back to the letter.

"Dear Hunter, Apologies for the lateness of a response. I read with interest your application for the internship position at my gallery and private studio. Your portfolio was intriguing. As you know, the gallery I am working with is trying to attract more Americans. Your fluency in French as an American was unique and certainly helped your resume. With your acceptance, the position will start the beginning of November.

Although I regret that we cannot offer you transportation, your room and board will be covered, along with the small stipend indicated in the application materials. Please respond as soon as possible. Sincerely, Isabelle Lebas."

Below the typed script was a small personal note: "Dear Hunter, Unfortunately, the only student housing units are a half hour train ride from the studio. However, I am pleased to offer you a small, comfortable room in my own home. You will find it is within walking distance to both the gallery and the studio. Best, Isabelle."

Amber stood and moved lethargically to her room. The perfume was making her head ache. She wasn't worried about having to move out. Hunter had already implied that she would simply be waiting for him. But who was this Isabelle Lebas? How old was she? Was she married? Who else lived in the house?

She knew she shouldn't be jumping to any conclusions. This was a wonderful opportunity for Hunter. So why did she feel like it was the end of her world?

Amber slipped on comfortable pajama pants and wandered back into the living room. She could hear Hunter banging around in his room. Curious, she listened outside his room to check to see if he was still on the phone. Finally, she knocked softly.

"Come in!"

Amber found Hunter sitting on the floor surrounded by several storage bins. He looked disheveled and ran his fingers through his unruly hair. In other words, he was insanely attractive.

"Sorry if I'm making too much noise. I can't find my passport."

"Oh, I was just reading. But I forgot to ask when you were supposed to leave."

Amber licked her lips nervously.

Hunter dug through one of the bins.

"Hmm? Oh, I'll try to arrive the week before I start. So probably the end of October."

He sighed and dumped one of the storage bins upside down on the floor.

"Sorry, Amber, but I've got to find this tonight."

"Sure. No problem." Amber padded over to him and gave him a chaste kiss on the cheek.

She would have liked to have kissed him passionately. But he was clearly not interested at the moment. She backed reluctantly out of the room.

"Good night! Hope you find the passport."

Amber lingered another moment by the door.

"Good night! Sleep well!"

Hunter responded automatically. He didn't even look up.

Amber plodded down the hall and stopped in the kitchen for another bottle of water. She stared at the fortunes from the cookies and felt a chill as she read them again.

First Hunter's. *A ship in harbor is safe, but that's not why ships are built.* It was as though his imaginary cookie fairy was trying to convince him to go away for new experiences. And that was great. Unless, of course, those new experiences led to Hunter falling for someone more exotic and sophisticated than she was. What if he got tired of dating someone with a trailer park background?

Amber sighed and contemplated her own fortune. If you want the rainbow, you have to tolerate the rain.

Ugh! If she hadn't seen the cookies wrapped in plastic she might have suspected that Hunter planted them there. But of course that was ridiculous. She knew that he hadn't anticipated the letter. That excitement was real.

Amber grabbed a cold bottle of water and plodded down the hall to her own room. Wasn't there a lot involved getting ready for a trip like that? Hunter was going to have scant time for her. And what about his classes and the TA position? He couldn't just drop everything. Could he?

Grabbing her laptop, Amber climbed onto her bed. She pulled up her calendar and stared at the precious days remaining before Hunter left. With their class schedules and her new job, she and Hunter didn't see a lot of each other even now.

Maybe she could fly to Paris to visit while Hunter was there! Excitedly, she began searching for flights. Her joy was short lived.

More than a thousand dollars for one ticket? Might as well be ten thousand dollars, she thought miserably.

She crawled into the bed and found herself sniffling.

How had such a good day turned into such a lousy one so easily? She couldn't get past the feeling that something about this trip would cause her to lose Hunter.

Chapter 14

Amber groaned inwardly as she realized her line of customers was not getting any shorter. Although she was grateful to have a job, her feet were killing her after the double shift she had pulled the day before. Ringing up groceries was not the most glamorous job in the world. The paycheck, however, meant not having to depend on Hunter's generosity for food.

"Miss? I still have coupons."

The harried mom's frizzy hair fell from the sloppy bun on her head and clung limply around her face. The infant strapped in the front of the shopping cart opened his mouth and screamed. Her other child, a preschool boy, grabbed a fistful of candy and dropped the pieces in various bags in the cart.

"Now, Thomas, that was naughty."

Amber tried to work up sympathy for the exhausted woman. But she worried about the growing line at her station. All the cashiers got timed to improve the experience of the customer. This woman was ruining her averages.

Amber shifted on her feet. All the woman's groceries were bagged. Yet the woman stubbornly dug around in her purse for more coupons. The guy bagging groceries had already moved down the line. Amber was on her own.

She gave the next person in line an apologetic smile. He frowned and backed his cart out of the line, causing further grumbling by other customers behind him.

Finally, the woman handed over a bundle of coupons. Amber scanned each one patiently. Several were not for the right item. Those, Amber politely handed back with an apologetic smile.

"I'm certain that I purchased those things!" Oblivious to the giant line behind her, the woman rummaged through the bags.

"Oh, how did this get in here?"

She fished out several pieces of candy and lined them up on the conveyor belt.

Amber rang up each piece the woman handed her. Out of the corner of her eye, Amber noted her supervisor watching with a frown. Ugh! As though she could make this woman move any faster. Finally, the woman paid and began moving away.

Her little boy, however, saw an opportunity. In full sight of Amber, he stared at her defiantly as he scooped up another fist of candy.

"I'm sorry. But you can't have that unless you pay for it first," Amber said in what she hoped was a firm, kid-friendly voice.

The little boy smiled and started to follow his mother.

"Hey, Miss!" Amber tried to get the mother's attention.

Glancing over, she saw her supervisor frown and jot something on her clipboard.

Amber leaned over and tried to stop the little boy, but he simply angled away from her. Great! What was she supposed to do now? Tackle the little shoplifter?

Then, suddenly, the boy found he couldn't move. A man had stepped deftly around him to block the kid's escape.

Amber's eyes widened as she recognized Hunter.

"Hey, little guy!" Hunter squatted next to the child.

"You forgot to pay the nice lady."

The little boy pouted sullenly.

"My mom already paid," he said, his little voice indignant.

Amber's supervisor watched curiously.

"Ah, but that was for the food in her cart. If you want more stuff, we need to go and ask your mother for more money."

Hunter spoke pleasantly. He even smiled.

Amber looked anxiously at the mother. She was busy trying to quieten the infant. The baby's face was scarlet. Amber was certain the kid could pass for a role in an exorcist movie. The infant's tiny back arched unnaturally as it writhed in the car seat.

That surely could not be normal, Amber thought. Other customers maneuvered their carts in a wide berth around the woman. Some people looked sympathetic. However, several looked as alarmed as Amber felt.

"No! This candy is mine." The little boy stared at Hunter as though daring him to say otherwise.

"No," Hunter said, his voice even. "Everyone around you, including me and the nice cashier, saw you take candy after your mother paid. So the candy is not yours."

The little boy threw the candy on the ground.

"I think you dropped that," Hunter said, his voice still even but commanding enough that even Amber felt a bit nervous.

His earlier smile was now gone. His eyes were dangerously bright.

"Why don't you pick up the candy and put it back where it belongs?"

Amber nervously checked out her supervisor's face. The woman seemed to be holding in a smile.

"I've got plenty of time."

Hunter's voice was icy. He sat back on his heels, his piercing eyes never looking away from the boy's face.

The boy cast one hopeful glance at his mother. Finally, he carefully gathered up the pieces and put them back in their appropriate spots. He looked to Hunter for approval.

"Excellent! That's how a little man acts." Hunter smiled and got to his feet.

"Give me a high five!"

The little boy complied with a small grin.

"Now, let's tell the pretty lady that next time we won't try to take candy without paying for it."

The little boy looked stricken, but Hunter waited with an encouraging smile.

"I won't take candy anymore," the little boy whispered, his head low.

"Good job," Hunter said, rewarding the boy with another smile.

"Give me another high five and then go and help your mom."

The little boy slapped Hunter's hand and then galloped toward his mom. He tugged on her leg and tickled the baby's foot. The infant immediately stopped screaming.

Grabbing the little boy's arm roughly, the mother hurried out of the store, practically dragging her son along.

The remaining customers in Amber's line broke into applause. Hunter blushed and bowed low.

"So you're a child whisperer," Amber said with a grin, quickly ringing up Hunter's small basket of food.

"Among other things," Hunter replied with a smirk.

"I'd be happy to reveal them to you when your shift is finished." He handed her the exact amount of money for the groceries.

Amber felt herself flush.

"Five o'clock," she whispered, aware of her supervisor's curiosity.

"See you later. I don't want to linger and get you in trouble."

Amber forced her eyes on the next customer.

"Sorry about the holdup."

The elderly woman smiled mischievously.

"That's a keeper, honey. Don't let him out of your sight."

Amber giggled. "Um . . . Yeah . . . Thanks."

Amber was glad she was busy because it helped her to not think so much about Hunter. She couldn't wait to see him again.

At the end of her shift, she saw her supervisor approach.

"Oh, hello, Stacey," she said nervously.

She debated with herself whether she should bring up the incident with the little boy or not.

But Stacey inexplicably smiled warmly.

"I normally don't like to see boyfriends coming around, Amber. But your young man completely surprised me."

Stacey laughed.

"I wish I had recorded that little boy's face when he realized that he wasn't going to be allowed to get away with stealing candy."

Amber gaped. Stacey hadn't exactly been warm and fuzzy up to this point. This was the first time Amber had ever seen the woman crack a smile.

"Hunter does have a way about him," she said carefully.

"It's okay. I still don't like boyfriends hanging around my employees. But he seems like a good guy. More importantly, he turned around what could have been an ugly situation."

Stacey held out a clipboard and motioned to a piece of paper with Amber's name on it.

"Also, I just want to say that your customer service time is really improving."

"Thanks," Amber said, glowing.

Another employee called for assistance and Stacey turned away.

"Keep up the good work!" she called over her shoulder.

Amber clocked out with a smile on her face. Her feet were killing her, but she didn't care. In just a few minutes, Hunter would be waiting outside to pick her up. It had only been a week since she found out about Hunter's internship. She was making the most out of their limited time before he left.

As she left the crew room, her phone buzzed with a text message.

Exit through door near fruit and vegetable section. Proceed left three parking rows. Walk back twelve parking spaces. I'll be in the thirteenth spot.

Amber grinned. Sometimes Hunter was such a nerd. A very nicely put together nerd, she thought. But still a nerd.

The Ranger Rover was, of course, exactly where he said it would be. Hunter jumped out and ran around the car to open her door.

"Oh, my!" Amber said. "I'm getting the full gentleman treatment. What's the occasion?"

Hunter only smiled secretly and walked back to the driver's side.

Amber sank into the leather seat with a sigh. She smiled at Hunter as he slid into his seat and started the car.

"It feels so good to be sitting at last." Amber groaned as she slipped off her sneakers and wriggled her toes.

"Feet still sore from yesterday?" Hunter asked sympathetically.

"Yeah, but at least I have tomorrow off."

"Maybe you'll feel better once we get home." Hunter grinned.

"Do you have something in mind?"

Hunter looked over and winked.

"It's a secret."

"A secret?" Amber sat up straighter.

"Come on. Can't you even give me a hint?"

"Nope!" Hunter refused to even look at her.

"What about for a kiss?" Amber fluttered her eyes at him.

"Nope!" Hunter kept his eyes straight on the road.

Amber pouted. But all her efforts were wasted.

Hunter could be annoyingly stubborn.

Chapter 15

Amber hobbled behind Hunter, her feet killing her. She headed straight for her room, thinking to collapse on her bed. She opened the door and then stopped, mouth open.

A large bouquet of yellow roses, wrapped in a silky, purple ribbon, awaited her attention in a crystal vase on the small, antique dresser. She read the small note: "Thanks for being the best part of my life for the past four weeks. – Hunter."

Amber felt herself tearing up. She had been so caught up in her new job and Hunter's impending departure that she had lost all track of time.

Hunter appeared behind her.

"I can't believe you remembered." Amber blushed. "I have to admit the date slipped my mind."

"Technically, the official date is Monday. But I couldn't wait to celebrate. Especially since you don't have to get up early tomorrow for work."

Amber pressed her nose into the fragrant roses.

"I'm glad you didn't wait. These flowers are beautiful. And smell amazing."

She hobbled back over to him and rewarded him with a long kiss.

"You were right. I do feel better already."

Hunter nodded at her feet.

"Why don't you rest and prop your feet up before dinner."

"Sounds good," Amber said with a groan.

"I was planning on ordering pizza for dinner. Is that okay? It's not super romantic."

Amber smiled. "It's perfect."

Grabbing a magazine, she kicked off her sneakers, and sprawled on her bed. Within a few minutes though, she dozed off.

She jerked awake when Hunter tapped her shoulder.

"Shh . . . It's okay. But I've got something else for you in my room."

Hunter led her to a chair in the middle of the room. A clean towel was spread out below it with a large, plastic bin of water.

"What's this?"

Hunter didn't answer. He left the room and came back with a steaming kettle. He poured the boiling water into the plastic tub, testing the temperature with his fingers. Finally, he left to put away the kettle.

As she peered at the steaming water, Amber thought about how good it would feel on her feet. And then she realized that was exactly what Hunter had intended.

Hunter came back with a box of Epsom salts and settled at her feet. He slowly peeled off her socks.

Just the touch of his fingers on her foot sent a shiver up her spine. Amber was surprised at how sensual it felt. As he pressed her feet into the tub, she felt the first relief from her aches as the heat quickly moved up her legs.

Hunter scooped up a handful of the Epsom salt, lifted one foot, and rubbed firmly just over her arch. Oh, that felt nice! It was if he knew exactly where her worst aches were stored.

She would have never imagined that a foot massage could be romantic. But it was just like Hunter to anticipate what she needed the most. She couldn't even imagine most guys would want to serve their girlfriends like this. And that in itself made the act romantic.

Chapter 16

"I'm going to go order dinner. Stay put if you want."

Amber flexed her feet in the cooling water and stretched. She finally stood, grabbed her dirty socks, and padded to her room. She took a quick shower and dressed in a pair of fresh jeans and a tee shirt.

When she entered the kitchen, she was surprised to see Hunter pulling out a couple of wine glasses.

"I didn't know that you even drank."

Hunter grinned and pointed at the bottle of sparkling cider.

He poured two glasses and brought them over.

"To us!" He raised his glass.

"To us," Amber repeated, raising her own glass and clinking it against Hunter's.

Once the food arrived, Hunter and Amber ate side by side on the sofa. But when they finished, Hunter reached behind one of the cushions and casually dropped a small box in her lap.

"What's this?"

Oh, wow. She hadn't gotten him anything at all.

Amber opened the box and began to laugh. Inside, resting on delicate pieces of pink tissue, were three plastic vials of glucose pills.

"I don't want you to pass out at work if you don't have time to eat."

Hunter reached over and picked up one of the containers.

"Here, try one now and see how it tastes. Supposedly, it's like candy."

Amber giggled. "That's okay. I'll just stick them in my purse."

"No, I insist." Hunter put the vial in her hand. "Open it right now!"

Amber frowned.

"Okay, Hunter, you have got to get over this pushy attitude."

She picked up the vial and aimed it at his head. Wait. What was that noise? The vial rattled.

"Hey, is something else in here?" She looked over at Hunter.

He looked angry.

"This better not be tampered with. Maybe I should take it back to the store."

He reached to take the vial from her.

"Wait. I want to see what it could be!"

Amber pulled away and bolted off the sofa.

Hunter stood up, grabbing for her.

She eluded him and ducked behind the kitchen table. Giggling, she popped the vial open and shook it over the table. And gasped.

Out fell a glittering emerald bracelet.

"Oh, my gosh! Hunter, it's beautiful!" A

Amber squealed and held the bracelet up to the light so she could watch it sparkle.

"You really had me going."

"Here, let me put it on you."

Hunter fastened the bracelet, lifted her hand up, and kissed her wrist.

Amber moved her arm away and substituted her mouth. She gave him her own gift of a kiss.

Chapter 17

Amber woke up late the following morning. She found Hunter bustling around in the kitchen as he prepared an elaborate breakfast.

"Whoa! Are you okay?" Hunter asked, looking up from a pan of sizzling bacon.

"Headache," Amber grunted.

She couldn't explain that she had woken in the middle of the night convinced that Hunter was going to forget all about her once he got to Paris. She had spent half the night staring at the ceiling, unable to sleep.

"Ah, I probably shouldn't have given you that second glass of sparkling cider. Who knew you couldn't handle your fake alcohol?"

Hunter turned off the gas burner and moved to the refrigerator.

"Let me get you a glass of juice and some aspirin."

Amber slumped at the table. She swallowed the aspirin and drained the glass. With her throbbing head and fatigue, she was in a foul mood. Worse, she was wasting precious time with Hunter before he left.

"Here, come sit on the sofa while I make you a nice cup of tea."

Amber felt herself softening. How could she question Hunter's loyalty when he treated her like this?

"Put your feet up here." Hunter adjusted the cushions behind her back and kissed her gently on the forehead.

"I'm sorry, Baby," he said. "It's my fault. I wasn't thinking. You needed your rest last night."

If only he would say that he had made a mistake and could not live even one week without her. But that was not going to happen. She knew she was being unreasonable. After all, they had only known each other for a month. She sighed.

Hunter went back to the kitchen and started to crack eggs in a bowl. Once he had finished preparing breakfast, he served her on the sofa.

Three cups of tea restored her energy. And the aspirin finally kicked in and erased the headache. She felt herself perk up. She might need a nap later, but she could certainly power through the day.

After she ate, Amber excused herself to check her phone messages. She saw a text from her supervisor asking if she wanted more hours. Two employees were no shows that morning. Amber ignored the messages. Hopefully, Hunter would have something fun planned for the day. She was determined to make the last few weeks pleasant.

"I'm feeling one hundred percent better," she announced with a smile.

She stood behind Hunter and gave him a hug as he finished cleaning up the breakfast dishes.

"That's great." He looked looked relieved.

"Um . . . I know we usually do something on Sundays, but I told Ben that I would meet him for lunch. I feel terrible for deserting him in the middle of the term like this."

"Oh, okay." Amber's stomach clenched. "Actually, my supervisor wants me to come in and cover for a no-show."

She secretly hoped that Hunter would feel bad and invite her to the lunch. Instead, he smiled.

"Oh, good. So you won't be bored all day. What time are you supposed to be there?"

Amber forced a smile on her face.

"Now is fine," she said. "I'll just send my supervisor a text that I'll be there in a few minutes."

Well, this was not the leisurely Sunday she had imagined. Amber headed to her room for her phone and ID badge.

The store parking lot was packed so Hunter stopped in the loading zone.

"Later, Gorgeous." He noticed her bracelet and smiled.

"Remember, green is for jealousy!" He winked, and she fell into those mesmerizing eyes.

Amber softened again. She leaned over and gave him a passionate kiss.

"Whoa!" Hunter pulled away, flushing. "Any more of that and you'll be late for work."

"Just don't want you to forget about me."

Amber pulled away reluctantly and grabbed her purse. She didn't trust herself to say anything else. So she just hopped out of the car and blew him a kiss. She didn't allow herself to watch Hunter drive away.

"Thanks so much for coming in. You are a life saver today," her boss gushed once Amber met her by the registers.

"I'll remember this when you need some time off."

Well, at least Stacey was grateful. The truth was that Amber did want to take a few days off around Christmas break. Maybe this would help. She hurried to the break room to clock in.

The store was packed and carts jammed the aisles. Taking a deep breath, Amber marched up to her register and punched in her access code. This was just what she needed to keep her mind off of Hunter.

A couple of hours later, Stacey came over.

"I'll cover your line for you," she said. "Take a break now while you can."

Amber headed for the break room, wishing she had thought to bring a snack. She could always buy something, but she didn't feel like waiting in one of the lines herself.

She looked in her purse for change. At least there was a soda machine in the break room. She fished in the bottom and laughed as she pulled out one of the vials of glucose pills. Okay, so Hunter had not been entirely kidding when he purchased them. He must have dropped these in her purse this morning.

Another employee, an older woman, was sitting at the break table when Amber walked in. She looked up and studied her name tag.

"I'm Sonia," she said. "A handsome young man with dark hair asked me to put a lunch sack in the fridge for you."

"Oh! Well, um . . . Thanks, Sonia." Amber smiled at the woman and then checked the refrigerator.

Just as Sonia said, there was a paper sack with her name on it. Amber pulled it out and saw that Hunter had packed a deli sandwich, apple slices, and a zip-lock bag with her favorite animal cookies. Underneath, he had also placed two cold bottles of water.

"That's some boyfriend you got there," the woman said, sounding envious.

She turned back to her book.

"Thanks! I think so too." Amber took a large bite from her sandwich.

Sonia was reading a romance book with a bare-chested man on the front cover. While she read, she was nibbling an egg salad sandwich and washing it down with a cup of coffee. Her ring finger was conspicuously bare. Had Sonia ever known love?

Amber had a sudden vision of herself at Sonia's age. Had she stayed with her mom, Amber might have ended up in similar circumstances. Had this woman known a hard childhood as well?

Sonia looked up, as though feeling that Amber was staring.

"Um . . . Is that a good book?" Amber said to cover her embarrassment at having been caught snooping.

Sonia considered her.

"It's a way to escape the real world. You know?"

"I suppose," Amber said, feeling awkward.

She wanted to throw away the rest of her sandwich but felt uncomfortable doing so in front of Sonia. To be honest, only a few weeks ago she would have been horrified to see someone throw away food. Had she changed so much already?

That was a sobering thought. Amber forced herself to finish every bite. She saved the apple slices and cookies for later. She was tempted to offer the cookies to Sonia but thought better of it. She was sure that Sonia would take it as an insult.

Then, as quickly as she could put the bag in the fridge, she politely excused herself. She couldn't wait to get back to work where it would be hard to think.

Chapter 18

The next several weeks passed much too quickly. Before Amber was mentally prepared, it was time for Hunter to leave. She opened her eyes sleepily and found Hunter staring at her, his emerald eyes soft.

"Good morning," he whispered.

"And good morning to you," Amber whispered back.

If only she could freeze time and they could stay here together.

Hunter sat next to her and seemed content to cuddle without speaking. The moment was only ruined after Amber's traitorous stomach rumbled and gurgled.

"All right, all right," Hunter said at last, laughing and kissing her cheek. "I'll get us some food."

As Hunter left the room, she snuggled lazily in the covers, thankful that at least she had not been scheduled to work that day. She couldn't believe that it had only been a matter of weeks since she had moved in as a roommate. The guys had been great about making her feel welcome.

Of course, now Hunter was going away for twelve weeks. An ache filled her chest. She already missed him and he wasn't even gone yet. Her eyes misted as she peeked out her bedroom door and saw Hunter slicing the tops off strawberries at the kitchen counter.

She didn't want Hunter to think she was emotionally unstable. She closed her door and headed to her bathroom. She turned the shower on full blast and stepped in, not allowing the water to warm first. Maybe icy water would shock her out of her moodiness.

The water was so cold that she had to suppress a yell. She gasped, not able to breathe regularly. The water was freezing. But it worked. By the time the water warmed, Amber had control of her emotions. In addition, she was fully awake. She showered quickly, not wanting to waste any of her precious time with Hunter.

By the time she finished, Hunter was sitting on the sofa flipping through a magazine, his hair damp and a small smudge of shaving cream behind one ear. A breakfast tray rested on the leather ottoman.

"And here I thought I was being quick in the shower."

Amber plopped down beside Hunter and picked up a strawberry.

"If you didn't dry your hair, you could compete with my time."

Hunter flipped his hair so that one floppy wet strand drooped over his forehead.

Amber was actually quite jealous of Hunter's thick, luxurious hair. He could simply get out of the shower, run a comb or his fingers through it, and still manage to look awesome.

"Oh, like that would be attractive," Amber said. "I'm sure you would appreciate me looking like a drowned rat while my hair dried."

Hunter leaned over and kissed her softly.

"But you would be my little drowned rat."

"Hmm . . . I don't think so."

Amber reached for another berry. She was hungry, but didn't feel like eating. But she had to admit that sitting here, eating breakfast with Hunter, now seemed like the most natural thing in the world. It was incredible how fast she had felt comfortable here in the apartment. Indeed, she had quickly allowed herself to forget about how dire her circumstances used to be.

The previous week she had watched with growing sadness and apprehension as Hunter methodically packed his luggage. Hunter's impending absence was bringing back some feelings she would have rather kept shoved in the back of her mind.

She shook her head, trying to clear it. This was supposed to be quality time with Hunter. She watched him as he chewed slowly, caught up in an article. She stared at him hard, trying to memorize every angle of his face so that she could think of him clearly while he was gone.

Suddenly he looked up, startled.

"What, do I have something on my face?"

Amber flushed.

"Um . . . No, I was just thinking about you not wearing jeans and tee shirts for twelve weeks." She smiled. "I'm going to need physical evidence to believe you're really wearing a suit and tie every day."

Hunter laughed.

"Yeah, well, I need to at least fake being a professional. And I suppose it's good practice for when I graduate."

Graduation. Amber hadn't put too much thought into that. Well, here was one more thing for her to worry about.

"Will you still be on schedule to graduate next spring?" she asked, hoping he would say no.

Hunter smiled.

"I was so busy getting things together this week that I forgot to tell you. I'm going to get credit for my classes after all. As long as I finish my portfolios while I'm gone, and have Isabelle write critiques, both Ben and Professor Stevens will give me credit."

Amber feigned a matching smile. "That's wonderful!"

Inside, though, she was wondering where that left her once Hunter finished school. Perhaps a place to live if she got roommates. She couldn't even get her head around this relationship being permanent. Her secret fear was that Hunter would wake up one day and realize that he could have another girl – a girl who didn't come with a trailer park, beer drinking, welfare abusing mom.

"Hey, pay attention!" Hunter teased, tugging on a lock of her hair.

"You look like you're a million miles away."

"Sorry," Amber said, smiling up at him. "Must be hunger related. Didn't you hear my stomach rumbling a little while ago?"

"I could have heard that little belly roar in Paris." Hunter examined the breakfast tray.

"You've only eaten a couple of strawberries. No wonder you're still hungry."

Tossing aside his magazine, he picked up a multi-grain bagel and slathered it with cream cheese.

"Open up," he commanded sternly.

Amber stared at the tray. Had Hunter actually counted the berries and bagels? But she couldn't refuse when he looked so anxiously at her like that. She obediently took a small bite and took the bagel from him.

Hunter stared at her with those hypnotizing eyes until he could have asked her anything at all and she would have complied.

"Promise me that you'll eat properly while I'm gone."

"Okay, okay!" Amber said, laughing.

She put her bagel down and impulsively threw her arms around Hunter's shoulders. She put her lips to his ear.

"I get the message. Do you realize that this is the third time in two days I've had to promise you the same thing?"

Hunter reached up to cup her face in his hands.

"I'm going to miss you something fierce," he whispered, his voice husky.

"It's going to be a long twelve weeks."

Amber tilted her head and kissed him slowly on the lips.

The alarm on Hunter's cell phone went off.

For about the hundredth time, she wanted to smash it to bits.

"The car service will be here in a few minutes to take me to the airport," Hunter said as he turned off the alarm.

"But before I go, I want to give you something." He pulled out a small card from his pocket.

"What's this? I already have your address there."

Then she looked more closely and saw that it was a car insurance card.

"I don't understand."

"I added you to my policy," Hunter explained, grinning. "So now you can drive the Range Rover."

Amber gaped at him.

"Wow, Hunter, that's huge. Are you sure you trust me?"

A flicker of doubt crossed Hunter's face.

Amber quickly amended her comment.

"I mean, I'm a good driver!"

She snatched the card before he could have second thoughts.

"I get to drive the Range Rover!"

"You'll drive carefully, right?" Hunter sounded nervous.

"No scratches or dings or dents?"

Amber kissed him. "Don't be a worry wort!"

A horn blared outside.

Amber thrust herself forward and gave Hunter a tremendous hug.

"You'll be great! Have fun, but not too much fun, and I'll see you in twelve weeks."

Hunter gave her a lingering kiss and then backed away slowly with a wide grin on his face.

"That's the way I want to remember you, Gorgeous." He picked up his bags.

"That's how I'll picture you in my dreams."

Then, just like that, he was out of the door. The silence in the apartment was overwhelming.

Amber rushed to the living room window. Hunter had just given his bags to the driver and was now looking up as though waiting for her.

She pressed her face to the window, hoping that he could see. He did, a smile lighting up his face. He gave her a small wave and then got into the car. Amber held her hand up to the window until the car had left the driveway. She knew it was ridiculous, but she felt as though her heart was breaking.

Chapter 19

After Hunter left, Amber cleaned the entire apartment. Not that it needed a cleaning, but she needed physical activity to keep her mind off of Hunter. However, all she could think about was the feel of his kiss on her lips and his green eyes locked with her own. An hour later, she was forcing herself to plow through her history text while she finished off the tray of fruit and bagels.

Even with a reduced class load, she had fallen behind in her reading. Thankfully, her sketchbook was up to date. Hunter had given her daily assignments to make sure that she stayed ahead, even with her new part-time job. As much as she grumbled when he tried to manage her time, Amber had to admit she got more accomplished.

After a couple of hours, she checked her phone for messages. Nothing. Even though Hunter had said that he probably wouldn't contact her until after his plane landed in Paris the following day, she had hoped for at least a text. She pushed the phone away and got up to get a drink from the refrigerator.

When she opened the fridge, though, she started to laugh. Neat rows of paper sacks, all labeled with her name and the contents inside, filled up one entire shelf.

Was this a good thing? Should she be concerned that he was so controlling that even her work snacks were planned in advance? Or was she an idiot not to appreciate this level of attention from a boyfriend?

Sighing, she shut the fridge. She suddenly realized that there was only one person she wanted to talk to other than Hunter.

With a guilty pang, she thought of the scant conversations she had made time for with Hannah. Her best friend! Grabbing her phone, she dialed Hannah's cell phone number.

Hannah picked up before the third ring.

"Well, if it isn't the elusive Amber Holloway! Please tell me that the infamous guy in your life is the reason or I'll be really angry."

Amber giggled. "I know. I know. I've been terrible and now I'm working too."

A half hour later, Amber had updated her friend with all the details, including Hunter's present absence.

"That reminds me," Hannah said. "I was hoping to hang out a bit with you during Christmas break. You're still coming to my house Christmas Eve, right?"

"Absolutely! Maybe you could stay a night or two with me. I'm sure Hunter wouldn't mind you staying over."

Hannah was silent a moment.

"Um . . . Any chance that I could bring someone as well?"

"Are you dating someone new too?" Amber asked eagerly. "Tell me all about him."

"Uh, I'm going to have to get off the phone."

"Oh, okay," Amber said, disappointed.

They used to talk for hours. This phone conversation felt forced.

"So I'll be bringing a guest to stay when I see you," Hannah repeated.

"I'd have to get Hunter's approval," Amber said. "I mean, I'm sure he wouldn't mind you staying. But he might object to a guy he hasn't met before."

She didn't add that she wasn't that keen on having a strange man staying over herself. Hannah wasn't known for picking the nicest guys in the world to date.

"Hey, we can talk later, sweetie," Hannah said, now sounding like she just wanted the call to be over.

The two girls spoke for a few more minutes. Hannah continued to be vague about school and the mystery boyfriend. Amber hung up feeling oddly depressed. She could feel that she and Hannah had definitely grown further apart.

But a visit from Hannah would definitely help take the sting out of Hunter's absence. Surely Hannah could understand that one guy wouldn't want another guy in his own house in his absence.

Amber grabbed her history book and notes and got to work. If she couldn't get time off from work, she at least needed to be ahead with her schoolwork. Both her final exam in History, and her final art projects, were due after the Christmas holidays.

She was still hard at work when she heard the Ranger Rover pull up. Caleb had taken it that morning for work. Remembering the insurance card, Amber smiled as she thought about being able to drive Hannah about in style.

Caleb was whistling off key when he came through the doors.

"Hi, Caleb!"

Amber wondered if she could come up with an excuse to drive the Range Rover somewhere. It had been ages since she had driven. Hunter had never offered her the opportunity prior to this.

"Hey, Amber. Did Hunter get picked up on time?"

"To the minute. Almost as though they knew that he would go ballistic if they were even one minute late."

Caleb grinned.

"Oh, I'm sure it's the same car service he always uses. They probably have a file just for Hunter."

"I bet it's several inches thick," Amber said, laughing.

"I bet the drivers draw straws to see who has to pick him up."

Caleb dropped his backpack on the floor and headed for the refrigerator.

Amber watched him, curious as to what he would say about the bags of snacks.

Caleb took one look and then twisted his head back to look at Amber. He sighed.

"I wish I could say that this surprises me."

Amber walked over and they studied the typed labels together.

"So . . . Are we going to just pretend that this is normal behavior?"

Caleb shrugged and tucked one fist beneath his chin.

"I look at it this way. Hunter is a confirmed control freak."

Amber nodded her head in agreement.

"But on the positive side, he isn't involved in the mafia." Caleb grinned.

Amber laughed and nudged him.

"Okay, so ignoring the control freak behavior it is."

Caleb suddenly looked stricken and began to root through the fridge.

"Hey, he didn't leave anything in here for me!" He sniffed dramatically.

"He finds the one girl of his dreams and then casts me aside like a . . . like a . . . like an old cell phone!"

"Aw, poor thing!" Amber couldn't wait any longer.

"Why don't I take you to get some cheap, fast food for dinner." She smacked the insurance card down on the counter.

"I feel a need to take the Range Rover for a spin."

Caleb's eyes gleamed. "I know just the place."

He looked around as though expecting someone to overhear them.

"A certain someone who shall remain unnamed always stops me from eating there."

"Really? There must be some incredible, mouth watering, greasy food there."

Amber grinned.

"Enough to give somebody a heart attack," Caleb said happily.

"And there is nothing that a certain person can do to stop us!" Amber gave Caleb a high five.

"Just give me a second to grab my purse. I'm starving!"

An hour later, Amber groaned as they headed back home.

"Ugh! I'm starting to question our sanity in eating there."

Caleb looked up, apparently not feeling much better.

"It was a difficult job. But it had to be done," he said grimly. He belched loudly.

"Um . . . Excuse me!"

Amber laughed.

"I agree the meal had to be eaten. And it was excellent until it hit my stomach."

She rubbed her belly.

"But I think I'm starting to appreciate the wisdom of Hunter's meal plans."

Caleb clapped his hands over his ears.

"No! I refuse to be indoctrinated!"

Amber laughed. Her stomach wasn't feeling great. But it was certainly in good enough shape to take the long way home. The Range Rover was proving to be a pleasure to drive.

Chapter 20

The first day of art class without Hunter was awful. Amber never realized how much she cherished the odd little moments when he would simply walk by her easel and brush against her elbow or share a secret smile. The new TA, Jessica, was nice enough. If Amber was being fair, she would have admitted that Jessica's quiet, thoughtful comments were quite perceptive. But of course, Amber wasn't being fair because she didn't want Jessica.

She wanted Hunter, plain and simple. She wanted Hunter's mesmerizing green eyes that made her melt beneath his gaze. She wanted to press her head against his taut chest. She ached to run her fingers through his thick, wavy hair. Even the paint and turpentine smell of the classroom reminded her of Hunter.

Professor Collins took off his glasses, pulled a handkerchief from his back pocket, and carefully polished the lenses.

Wow, Amber thought, seeing him without glasses for the first time. Professor Collins was one hot tamale! She looked sideways at Megan.

Megan held up two thumbs and winked.

"Let's do something a little different today," Professor Collins said, unaware of the new tension he had just created in the classroom.

"Break up into pairs and let's work on faces."

Megan immediately dragged her easel over. This was a rare opportunity for the two girls to talk during class time.

"I guess we're pairing up?" Amber teased.

She turned her easel so that she faced Megan.

As she studied her friend, Amber noted for the first time just how pretty Megan was. She would make a great model. Her skin was so smooth and pale it was almost translucent. A soft sprinkle of freckles trotted across her nose. Electric blue eyes. Delicate, pale lashes. She didn't seem to want or need even a drop of makeup. A cascade of brilliant red curls draped her face.

"I know Hunter's internship must be tough for you," she said sympathetically. "If you ever want to hang out, just give me a call."

"Thanks, I really appreciate that. Are things okay with you? You look a bit tired."

Amber knew that Megan was struggling just to keep up in class. She worked as a waitress in one of the local restaurants in town most nights and weekends.

For a moment, Amber felt a bit guilty. She would be in Megan's position if it were not for Hunter's generosity. She still couldn't believe how quickly her own life had turned around.

"I could really use a whole day to sleep," Megan said ruefully.

"I can help. I've got notes up to chapter 20. I'll e-mail them to you tonight."

Megan brightened.

"That would be awesome! I've only had time to skim over the material before class."

Amber shrugged with an embarrassed smile.

"It's a lot easier for me this semester because I'm only taking the two classes. Even with work, I've got a lot more time on my hands than you do."

Jessica frowned in their direction so the two girls settled down and got to work. Amber became so engrossed that she was still working on her sketch of Megan after the bell rang.

Megan waved as she hurried off to her next class.

The art room was empty now. Even Professor Collins had returned to his office. Amber wasn't even sure why she was lingering. She slowly gathered her things and prepared to leave. But before she got to the door, she was surprised to find Kayla waiting just outside.

Kayla who looked like a model. Kayla with nails painted like bloody talons. Kayla who hated her guts.

Amber immediately flashed back to her last encounter with the girl. Kayla had been furious to discover that Hunter was dating her. Amber had assumed that Kayla had moved on to lick her wounds somewhere else. But now she was here. Was it a coincidence that she showed up the very first day that Hunter was gone? Of course not.

Chapter 21

Kayla sauntered into the room and casually sat on the corner of Professor Collins' desk. Crossing her slim legs, she placed both hands primly on her knees. She wore high heels which clashed considerably with her surroundings. When she smiled, Amber could see a smear of lipstick on her front tooth.

"Poor little Amber," she cooed. She made a sad face.

"You must be so lonely now that Hunter is away. I was surprised that you didn't tag along."

Amber knew she was being baited, but she couldn't help herself.

"It's an internship, Kayla. He's working there and I'm going to school here."

She shrugged her shoulders. "No big deal."

Kayla pursed her lips.

"Oh, but you must be looking forward to spending the holidays visiting the city with his parents. Paris is so beautiful any time of the year. But I think it's particularly romantic at Christmas. Don't you?"

Amber felt her pulse quickening, part with alarm and part with anger. Where was Kayla going with this? Of course Hunter would spend Christmas with his parent. But Kayla was acting as if she knew that Amber would not be there. How would she know?

Amber wanted to simply walk away. But she didn't want to appear weak.

"Hunter and I'll have our own special celebration when he gets back," she said, trying to keep emotion out of her voice.

"Oh, that's a shame!" Kayla's voice dripped with fake concern.

"And here I was hoping that you and I could meet up in the city of love and do a little shopping together."

She smiled, her eyes hard. "I know all the exclusive little shops. With a good hair dresser and some decent clothes, I bet you would be quite cute."

Amber tried to laugh off her embarrassment.

"Apparently Hunter likes my style. Since he's dating me."

Kayla smiled tightly. "Well, boys tend to put up with a lot for sex. At least in the beginning."

Amber wasn't about to walk into that trap. She put down her bag and dragged over a stool to sit on. She needed to move around so that Kayla couldn't see how much she was unnerving her.

Was Kayla really going to be in Paris for the holidays? Was something planned with Hunter's family? Or was Kayla simply lying again?

"So, Kayla, what's the point here? With you and me, I mean?"

Amber forced herself to sit upright. Sitting down was a huge mistake because now Kayla towered over her.

Kayla uncrossed her legs and smoothed her skirt with her fingers. She flexed her feet and the sequins on her heels glinted.

"Oh, sweetie, you have me all wrong," she said, with an exaggerated sigh. "I know I got off on the wrong foot with you."

Amber squinted at Kayla in confusion. Where was Kayla going with this? Was she really going to suggest that the two of them be buddies?

"Telling someone to keep their hands of their non-existent boyfriend tends to alienate people," Amber said dryly.

"Especially when it seems that there was never even a single date with the nonexistent boyfriend in question."

Kayla winced.

"I said some things I shouldn't have," she admitted. "Yes, I was jealous of Hunter's attention. You came out of nowhere and suddenly he was all over you."

Amber grew wary. She didn't trust Kayla as far as she could spit. What was she up to?

"You should understand that I've known Hunter since middle school."

Kayla palmed her skirt as though she was nervous. Her foot jerked up and down, making it hard to concentrate on her face.

"Hunter's dad hired my father to take over as the Chief Financial Officer. Naturally, we met at some functions. Our parents started hanging out and became good friends."

Amber heaved a sigh of frustration.

"Nice story. But what does this have to do with now? Hunter isn't even interested in working at his father's company."

Kayla's eyes narrowed. "Oh, don't be so sure about that. He is already on the Board of Directors there. So he has influence whether he talks about it or not."

Amber stood up. "So, you're telling me that Hunter is so interested in his father's business that he decided to get his degree in art? And then spends all his time drawing and painting?"

She picked up her things, preparing to leave. She couldn't believe she had allowed Kayla this much of her time.

"Be that as it may," Kayla said. "But I doubt if Hunter would ever do anything to bring down the image of his father's company."

She slid off the desk with a small smirk on her face.

"Still not getting your drift," Amber said, turning her back on Kayla, her bloody talons, and ridiculous high heels.

Who wore high heels to class, anyway?

"Oh, I can see the headlines one day," Kayla said evenly.

"Daughter of trailer trash to wed into wealthy Webb family. A regular Cinderella story."

Kayla's words were knife blades slicing through Amber. How had Kayla known? Had Hunter told her? Had the girl hired someone to search her past?

In spite of feeling like she was crumbling inside, Amber simply kept walking. When she spoke, it was with a fake strength and confidence.

"Get lost, Kayla!"

Behind her, Kayla laughed.

Amber had to fight not to run. She slipped out the front door and then backtracked to another side door. Escaping into an empty restroom, she barricaded herself into a stall and sobbed.

She had pushed away the thought that Hunter had not introduced her to his parents yet, telling herself it was much too soon in their relationship. But what if there was more to it than that?

Hunter was willing to forget about her past to date her. But could he put his family in the position that Kayla hinted at? Would she want that?

She reached up to wipe at her eyes and the fluorescent light caught on her bracelet, making it twinkle. Hunter had said that this bracelet was the sign that she was his one and only. Why had he given it to her if he was simply playing with her for the time being? If she believed Kayla, then she had to suspect Hunter's intentions.

She massaged her throbbing forehead with her fingers. Ugh! If she only had kept walking when she first saw Kayla. Sniffling, she got herself together. She washed up at the sink, splashing her face with cold water until her eyes were not so obviously red from crying.

Amber slipped quietly into the hallway, not wanting anyone she knew to see her tear-stained face. Fortunately, this side of the building was mostly offices. As she made her way down the long empty corridor, however, she was surprised to hear Kayla's voice again.

Ugh! What was Kayla still doing here? She wasn't even an art major.

Amber looked back, searching for a place to hide. She certainly didn't want Kayla to see that she had been crying.

There was nothing behind her but the candy and soda machines. Sprinting forward, Amber dodged to the side of the candy machine. Lucky for her, someone must have moved the machine to service it. Seeing an opening, she wedged herself in, smearing her shirt and jeans with what she hoped was dirt. A grease stain would ruin one of her favorite tee shirts.

Even though she knew she was hidden, Amber couldn't help but panic as she heard Kayla and another woman approach.

"Do you think it worked?" the other woman was saying.

"I don't know, Mom," Kayla sighed

"Hey, do you have some ones or change? I'm really thirsty."

"Go for the diet, dear. I've noticed you've put on a couple of pounds. You know Hunter likes the willowy look in a girl."

Amber's breath caught in her throat. Kayla's mom was involved? Weird!

"Oh, can you stop it already, mom?" Kayla wailed, sounding frustrated.

"I've done every single thing you've suggested to get him to like me. Nothing works! Face it. He's never going to fall for me!"

"I have not come this far to have everything taken from me, " Kayla's mom responded, her voice hard as steel.

"Stop this whining right now!"

"I don't know what you want me to do," Kayla said, her voice hopeless. "Why can't I find somebody else?"

"How many times do I have to tell you what is at stake here?"

"Why me?" Kayla shouted suddenly, her voice angry.

"I wasn't the one who screwed up. Why do I have to be the one to try to fix everything?"

Amber tried to keep her breaths shallow. She didn't know what was going on. But she didn't want to miss one second of this. Was Kayla's family in some kind of trouble? How in the world would dating Hunter help?

"Not one more word, Kayla! I'll meet you in the car. Your attitude better be changed by the time you get there."

There was the sound of heels clicking rapidly down the hall, moving away from the candy and soda machines. The doors whooshed open and then clanged shut again seconds later.

Amber fought the urge to sneeze. Her legs were cramping, and she was finally aware of a sharp corner poking her in the chest. She willed Kayla to follow her mother down the hallway.

Instead, Kayla started muttering to herself under her breath.

"Cold-hearted . . . Deserves to rot . . . See if I care . . . Should just leave . . ."

Finally, coins clanked in the machine. A mechanical whir was followed by a soft thump as a drink clanked to the bottom of the machine.

Okay, you got your drink, Amber thought. Now just go. She held her breath against the threat of another sneeze. She wasn't sure what would happen if Kayla found her back here. Awkward wouldn't even begin to describe what she would feel.

"Diet Coke, hah!"

Amber heard the pop of a soda can being opened followed by gulping. Just when Amber thought she was close to being free, she heard more money being fed into the machine. This time there were two separate thumps.

Amber noticed a shadow moving across the wall beside her. She panicked, trying to think of a plausible excuse. Maybe she could say that she dropped some bills. A draft sucked the money under the machine. She tried to reach under the machine but had gotten stuck.

Yeah, that was reasonable. Any two-year old would buy that. Sweat pooled under Amber's arms. She started to worry about any loose, frayed wires. She could see it now. Strange Girl Electrocuted While Hiding Behind Candy Machine. Wealthy Boyfriend Suspected Insanity.

But then she felt the machine jar as Kayla leaned against the machine and slid to the floor. Just great! From this close, she could hear Kayla rapidly chewing and swallowing. She wondered if Kayla had an eating disorder. The frantic way the girl was stuffing the food in her mouth was quite disturbing. At one point Kayla burped loudly. She was sitting so close that Amber could smell her chocolate and peanut butter breath. Finally, Kayla stood up and started walking down the hallway.

"Horrible shoes!" she muttered, her steps uneven.

Amber smiled. Kayla must have one horrible blister the way she was hobbling. And then she felt a moment of alarm. Whatever Kayla had done, or was planning to do, was nothing compared to what her mother was contemplating. She sounded desperate.

Amber had heard that level of desperation from her own mother when money was short and the rent was due. Could Kayla's family have financial woes? But wasn't the father some sort of bigwig executive type? None of this made sense.

Amber waited several minutes after hearing the building door shut. Then she slipped out of her hiding spot. She ducked back into the restroom to clean up. She stared at her image in the mirror. She now sported a ripped and stained tee-shirt. Her fingers were filthy, and she had managed to get a smear of oil on her cheek.

She sighed as she finally left the building. This had turned into a day to skip history class. She didn't think she could handle one more unpleasant experience in her day. Facing drool boy just wasn't an option.

Chapter 22

Amber quickly learned that trying to communicate with Hunter by phone was annoyingly difficult because of the time zone difference. Although he sent frequent texts, she barely got to speak to him in person. To make matters worse, Hunter texted the photograph that been printed in the gallery newsletter.

In the photo, Hunter stood proudly next to the stunning Isabelle Lebas. The raven haired woman, slender and leggy, wore a black form-fitting sheath and impossibly tall heels. She held one arm possessively around Hunter's shoulder. Hunter looked incredibly handsome in his suit and tie. His smile showed exactly how happy he was.

Amber had stared down at her frumpy pajama pants and old tee-shirt, feeling hopeless. How could she hope to keep Hunter's attention when he was tempted by a woman like Isabelle Lebas? She forced herself to write a lighthearted response: "Do not recognize the responsible adult in the photo. Please send search party for Hunter Webb."

She added a smiley face and hit send. Then, realizing that the reply might sound too flippant, she quickly added a second message. "Very proud of you! Sure that you are exceeding expectations." She hit reply a second time, wondering when he might see the message. It was now six o'clock in the morning his time.

After the photograph, Amber took as many shifts as her supervisor offered, often coming in to work when others were no shows. If she didn't have a class, Amber always went in. She even worked Thanksgiving morning, refusing Caleb's invitation to spend the holiday at his mom's house.

Hunter had not been happy over her missing Thanksgiving dinner. However, there was little he could do from Paris to make her change her mind. Of course, Stacey was so impressed that she promised to let Amber have several days off in a row during Christmas break.

Even though Kayla had not come around again, Amber was always looking over her shoulders, sure that the girl would pop up on her again when she was least prepared. Maybe that was even part of Kayla's strategy to keep her unnerved.

Knowing that Kayla was being forced to go after Hunter was not enough to keep Amber's anxiety levels down. In some ways it made things worse. If Kayla felt like she ultimately had no choice, she would always be trying to find a wedge that would cleave Amber and Hunter apart.

At least working double shifts and coming home exhausted helped Amber survive the lonely weekends. Painting was also a balm. She appropriated Hunter's room as her own private studio so that she didn't have to commute to the college after hours. She would stay there, painting late into the night. Professor Collins expected three finished paintings by the end of the term. Amber was determined that she would make a good impression. She had chosen some of her early sketches of Hunter to work with for one of the paintings.

The other two paintings, however, were self-portraits. She knew she was taking a risk, but she felt a deep need to search within herself. When she looked in the mirror, she saw only her flaws. She saw her mother's failures in life. She saw a girl who could easily be discounted. A girl who was easily broken.

Amber contrasted herself with both Isabelle Lebas and Kayla. Even in a photograph, Amber saw that Isabelle Lebas was a woman to be reckoned with. She stood straight. She stared at the camera with confidence.

And Kayla? Except for that one moment of weakness around her mother, even Kayla strutted around as though she owned the world. Perhaps that was what scared Amber the most. What if Hunter was attracted to another woman without her family baggage?

When Hunter was around, he made Amber feel strong and confident. But now that he was gone, she knew that she was reverting back to her timid self. She kept her head down at work and avoided problems. She felt most animated when she painted or sketched. She hoped to catch some of that essence in her self-portraits.

How could she expect Hunter to ever love her if she could not find something to love in herself? Maybe that was her ultimate downfall. She was jealous of the confidence other women had.

Perhaps Kayla was right. Perhaps her past was something that Hunter ultimately wouldn't be able to accept. But if that was the case, why seek out her affection in the first place? He knew all about her from the very beginning. Were his parents going to be an issue? Would she ever even meet them? Ugh! She wished she could stop her brain from thinking too much!

As Christmas break approached, she started anticipating Hannah's visit. Surely Hannah would see that they just needed a girl night or two to bond again. Amber was even curious about meeting the mystery guy. She was puzzled as to why Hannah was being so secretive. It simply wasn't like her at all. Hannah typically bragged about her recent conquests. Which made this particular guy seem a little scary to Amber. Was there a reason Hannah didn't want anyone to know about him?

Still, with all the extra shifts she had taken, she had saved enough to pay for a couple of dinners out. But just a week before Christmas, Amber was taken by surprise when Hannah announced that she was still bringing someone with her.

"Okay, I've been holding out," Hannah said. "But I want to bring John with me and I just don't think that Dad's going to like him."

"That's never stopped you before," Amber said.

Frank and Lucy were actually pretty liberal with Hannah. Boys could stay over as long as they stayed in the guest room.

"Yeah, well, I'm in college now. And John is a bit older, so he is not going to take kindly to sleeping in a guest room with me down the hall."

"So bring him for dinner and then get a hotel room. You don't even have to tell them you're still in town while he's visiting."

Hannah dropped her voice a notch.

"Um . . . The thing is that he's a bit short on cash. No big deal. But he needs a place to crash. So I figured we could just stay at your place until Hunter gets back."

"Until Hunter gets back? That's a couple of months from now! What about school?"

Hannah laughed. "Come on, what are you worried about? Hunter can afford it. I'm guessing he gives you money for groceries and bills. I've got it all figured out. You hire us as personal assistants. Drive you around. Buy your food, pay the bills. You pay us with a little beer money, room and board."

Amber stared at the phone. "You're joking right? You aren't even making sense! And, for the record, Hunter doesn't give me money."

"Stop being a goody two shoes, Amber," Hannah said, her voice sharp. "My family helped you out. Now it's time for you to help me out."

"Hannah, you know I'd help you out if I could. But you're talking about using Hunter. And there is no way he would allow two people to live in his apartment the whole time he was gone. Even if he would, my room isn't that big."

"Your room?" Hannah laughed.

"Oh, sweetie, I wouldn't want to displace you. We could use Hunter's room. You said it's the biggest room in the house."

Amber felt lightheaded. She couldn't believe that Hannah was even asking her this. She would have to be hopped up on drugs to be thinking this irrationally.

"Um . . . Hannah? You stopped taking the uppers, right?"

The other end of the phone got silent. For a moment, Amber thought that Hannah had hung up on her. Which meant that she was way off base. Or spot on target.

When Hannah finally responded, she sounded ticked off.

"I can't believe you're pulling this crap," she said harshly. "I thought we were friends."

"Oh, come on, Hannah," Amber retorted, suddenly angry herself. "You haven't seen me in months. Now you suddenly have this boyfriend that you can't bring home to your dad. The boyfriend is dead broke and you want me to hand over my boyfriend's apartment, money, and car? Do you even recognize how insane you sound?"

"I'm sorry, Amber," Hannah said, sounding contrite. "I'm just so caught up with John. I want to be with him so much. You know how that feels, right?"

"Of course I do, Hannah! You know how much it's killing me while Hunter is gone."

"Look, I have to go," Hannah said suddenly. "I'll see you at my parents on Christmas Eve and we'll work all this out then. Okay, sweetie?"

And just like that, Hannah hung up on her. Ugh! She had forgotten how stubborn Hannah could be. This trip was supposed to be a best friend get together. But she knew that Hannah would be fully absorbed with this loser guy John. Worse, she had a bad feeling that Hannah was using drugs again. Hannah had sworn to everyone that she was clean after a stint in rehab her senior year of high school.

Amber threw down the phone and rubbed her forehead. She could feel a headache coming on. She had a feeling that Hannah was going to try to force the issue. She didn't want to fight her best friend.

Later, Amber stared at her image in the mirror as she painted. Was standing up for herself wrong? Yes, she owed Hannah's family. But surely not this way. How was she going to fix this? She only had a few days to figure it out. And if Hannah was truly her friend, would she even be asking Amber to compromise her relationship with Hunter?

Chapter 23

Pulling up to the modest home where Hannah's parents still lived, Amber sat in the Range Rover for several minutes. For the first time, she felt uncomfortable coming here. Hannah's parents had been there for her ever since she could remember. She had often spent the night here when things got too rough at home. The past several years, she had celebrated at least Christmas Eve at their house. When they were younger, she and Hannah had been inseparable. But in high school things blurred a bit.

While Amber often worked to save for college, Hannah dated and enjoyed all that high school had to offer. When Amber wasn't working, she was studying late at night to keep her grades up. She knew that her only hope of escaping her mother's life was to go to college. The problem, she realized suddenly, was that she was outgrowing Hannah.

Sighing, Amber grabbed her small bag of gifts and carried them inside. Like always, she simply opened the front door and walked in. Hannah's parents would have been insulted if she had rung the bell.

As she entered the foyer, Amber was surprised to hear Hannah and her dad yelling. She stopped, not wanting to invade their privacy. She started to back up and go sit in the car for ten minutes when Hannah's mom, Lucy, stopped her.

"Amber, honey. Let me look at you!"

She waved a hand in the direction of the verbal fight.

"Don't mind them. They'll stop fussing in a few minutes. Frank is upset because of Hannah's grades."

Lucy opened her arms, and the two hugged for several moments.

"My, you get prettier every time I see you," Lucy said.

"Hang up your coat and let's go and stop all this racket. It's Christmas Eve and I'm not having it ruined with temper tantrums."

Amber squeezed her coat in the small closet and took off her shoes. She padded in her sock feet behind Lucy.

Lucy was a lion trapped in a tiny woman's body. Her temper was legendary. Amber grinned as Lucy grabbed a yardstick from the top of the refrigerator. When she and Hannah had been naughty as kids, Lucy would always grab that ruler and chase them around the house with it. She never actually touched them, but the threat always felt real. They always stopped whatever mischief they were involved in.

Now, Amber giggled as Lucy marched into Hannah's room, brandishing the yardstick like a sword.

"I thought I told you two to knock it off half an hour ago!"

Both Hannah and her dad, Frank, ducked and dodged, trying to move out of Lucy's path. It was particularly amusing because Frank was over six feet tall and had bulging muscles. Lucy, on the other hand, barely measured five feet and probably weighed no more than a hundred pounds.

"Now, Lucy, just calm down!" Frank used his forearm to block a whack on his chest.

"I told you that I just needed to have a little chat with Hannah about school and . . . Ow! Give me that before you hurt someone."

Frank finally wrestled the yardstick out of Lucy's hands.

"This is going in the trash."

Hannah, who had danced out of danger at the very beginning, laughed.

"Oh, Dad, you know she'll just get another one. I think they give them to her for free at the fabric store."

She suddenly noticed Amber standing in the hallway.

"Sweetie! I've been dying to see you!" She ran over and gave Amber a hug.

"I'm so glad you came!"

Later, after dinner was eaten and gifts had been exchanged, Hannah tried to talk Amber into staying until the next day.

But Amber had already promised Caleb the Range Rover by nine o'clock that evening. He was picking up his mom up for a Christmas Eve service. Although she lived just one town over, she had recently had surgery and couldn't drive herself.

"Oh, come on. Just have Caleb take a cab," Hannah whispered in the kitchen. "Dad confiscated my keys and I'm supposed to meet John later tonight."

Amber sighed with exasperation.

"So have John pick you up. And for the record, I'm not making Caleb take a cab back and forth from one town over. Do you know how much that would cost? And his poor mother just had surgery."

Hannah gripped Amber's shoulders, her eyes intense and disturbingly glazed.

"Amber, I'm asking as your friend," she said, her voice like a hiss.

Amber thought back to her first glimpse of Caleb, sweating and panting from running up three stories to her apartment after Hunter asked him to bring her food. That, she realized was what a friend did. A friend did not ask someone to do something like this. In fact, this was something that Hannah would have never asked of her in the past.

"Are you in trouble, Hannah?"

Hannah jerked her head back, seeing if her parents had heard.

"I'm fine," she said, her voice seething. "But I need transportation and I need it tonight."

"I'm sorry," Amber said. "In more ways than you can imagine. But I'm leaving right now."

Amber turned away from Hannah's shocked expression. Raising her voice, she called out her goodbyes to Lucy and Frank. They rushed out to hug her once more. Hannah stalked off to her room.

Pulling out of the driveway, Amber felt weird. She was sad about Hannah but also proud that she had stood up for herself. After seeing Hannah's condition, she was worried that her friend was dabbling in drugs. Maybe a few days home would help sober her up.

When Amber got home, an hour earlier than she had planned, she took Caleb up on his offer to attend the Christmas Eve service with his mom. Mrs. Hanson was a sweet woman. But on this night, she hounded poor Caleb as he drove to the service.

"You need to settle down with one nice girl like Amber. Stop flitting around from girl to girl like you're some worker bee gathering nectar from a million different flowers."

Amber suppressed her laughter with her hand as she caught Caleb's desperate looks in the rear-view mirror.

"Aw, Mom. Can we talk about this later?"

Once they got to the church, Mrs. Hanson finally dropped the subject.

The church was beautiful with tiny candles and huge garlands of greenery that draped the stained glass windows and the pews. Although they had arrived early, the pews filled up quickly. Amber wasn't surprised when a subdued voice asked her if the spot next to her was taken.

Absorbed in reading the service bulletin, she only glimpsed an expensive business suit and black dress shoes out of the corner of her eye.

She was shocked, though, when the person grabbed her hand. She looked up, gasping, and found herself staring into brilliant green eyes. And not just anybody's green eyes.

"Hunter . . . How . . . When?" she sputtered, trying to keep her shocked voice low.

Hunter leaned over, his eyes never leaving hers.

"I'll explain later," he whispered, his lips tantalizingly close to her ears.

Finally, he lifted his eyes and looked over Amber's shoulders to where Caleb sat with a satisfied smirk on his face.

"You knew," Amber whispered, her mouth open.

"Whew!" Mrs. Hanson said, suddenly reaching down and pulling off the big brace on her leg.

"That was getting a little uncomfortable." She reached across Caleb's lap and patted Amber's arm.

"We all knew but Hunter wanted it to be a Christmas surprise."

Awestruck, Amber blinked back tears.

"Hey! You can't cry when I'm your Christmas present!"

"Tears of joy," Amber mumbled, squeezing Hunter's hand. "I'm just a little overwhelmed."

"Me too."

Amber couldn't stop sneaking looks at him the whole service. Fortunately, the service itself was so beautiful that she forgot everything but the present. It was only when they stood to leave, and Hunter put a hand on the curve of her back, that she began to think about the rest of the evening.

After they had all piled into the car, Hunter drove Caleb and his mom home. Apparently, the whole visit was part of the ploy. Amber gave both Caleb and Mrs. Hanson giant hugs before they left.

And then, before she knew it, she was all alone with Hunter. At last.

He kissed her and then swirled her around as though they were in an old romantic movie.

"This is the best Christmas Eve!" Amber snuggled into Hunter's arms, wishing that she could stay there forever.

"A fireplace with a roaring fire would be nice right about now," Hunter said as they sat on the couch close to midnight.

"Agreed," said Amber. "But since we don't have one I think that we're going to have to keep making do with kisses."

Hunter grinned. "It's a hardship I'm willing to endure."

He leaned over and placed his lips over hers.

Chapter 24

The following morning, Hunter insisted on taking Amber out for a fancy Christmas buffet at a ritzy hotel.

"But I don't have anything to wear," Amber objected.

"Maybe you should open your Christmas gifts first, then."

Hunter led her into the living room.

A small, potted Christmas tree, decorated with twinkling blue lights and tiny, red and white bows stood on the coffee table.

"Where did this come from?" Amber asked, puzzled. "I know it wasn't here last night."

"I had Caleb put it in his room so I could surprise you this morning."

Propped up against the tree were a couple of brightly wrapped packages.

"Wait!"

Amber ran to her room and came back with her own small wrapped box.

"It isn't much," she said, as she placed it beside the gifts with her name.

"Baby, you could get me a pair of athletic socks and I would be happy. I'm just so thrilled to see you."

Amber made a pouty face as she sat on the sofa.

"But I spent a lot of time picking out those socks."

Hunter laughed.

"Let me open my gift first. I need some clean socks this morning."

Amber handed him the package and watched as he carefully untied the bow. He slid one finger under the first piece of tape and tugged gently.

"Um . . . Hunter?"

"Yes, gorgeous?"

"What are you doing?"

"Opening my package?" Hunter looked confused.

"Oh, never mind."

Amber watched as Hunter meticulously removed the paper and set it aside. She bit her lip, hoping he would like the gift.

"These are awesome!" Hunter grinned when he saw the small pile of brushes lying in pale, blue tissue paper.

He leaned over and kissed her before holding up each individual brush to inspect and admire.

Amber watched him with an insane grin on her face.

"But," he said hesitantly. "These are insanely expensive. Please tell me you didn't get a credit card."

"Nope! Paid for in cash!" Amber bragged. "I've been working a lot of extra shifts at the store."

Hunter smiled, obviously relieved.

"Then I'm going to enjoy them even more." He gave her a long kiss.

When Hunter handed her his gifts, she grinned mischievously.

"Now this is how you open a present," she said, ripping with gusto.

Bits of paper flew everywhere. Hunter laughed and backed away in mock alarm.

Inside the first box was a pair of black, knee-length, soft leather boots.

"Oh, they're so lovely!"

Amber immediately took them out of the box and put them on, standing to test the fit. They were perfect.

Hunter patted the sofa beside him and held out the next box.

Sitting down, Amber gave him an excited kiss on the cheek and then tore into the next package. This one held a beautiful, gray, well-cut dress with half sleeves and a simple bodice. Just by looking, Amber knew it must have been terribly expensive.

"Hunter, this is a lot," she said. "I love it. But you spent so much money on me."

Hunter smiled. "What? This old thing? Got it on clearance at Macy's."

He prodded her and pointed to his watch.

"Now, go and get changed quickly so that we aren't late for brunch. We have reservations."

Amber stood and saluted. "Yes, sir!"

Then she wriggled her hips as she walked to her room. When she returned, wearing the new dress that hugged her curves perfectly, along with the new boots, she found Hunter looking incredibly handsome. In fact, he looked like a model.

"Wow, I feel like we're actually adults." Amber smiled. "You look amazing."

"Thank you, my dear."

Hunter tucked his hands in his pockets and spun around. His gray, fitted dress pants hugged his hips. A pin-striped button-down shirt, with the top three buttons unfastened, looked as though it was molded to his chest. He held a matching gray jacket over one shoulder.

He held the other arm out to her.

"You look insanely beautiful in that dress, Miss Holloway. You are making it incredibly difficult for me to stick to our kisses only arrangement."

A half hour later, Amber caught her reflection in the mirrored hall of the hotel. *Is that really me?*

She hardly recognized herself. She looked sophisticated and beautiful. For perhaps the first time, she felt worthy of Hunter. At least for this moment, Hunter was all hers.

As they ate, Hunter told her about his life in a house with rambunctious four-year-old twins. Isabelle Lebas was apparently a devoted wife to her jolly husband and her small children. Amber realized how crazy she had been to suspect someone she had never met. Worse, she realized that she had not trusted Hunter. All of her jealousies had been over a phantom seductress who never existed.

Later, as Hunter admired her self portraits, Amber was able to look at them with fresh eyes.

"I can see how your emotions changed from portrait to portrait," Hunter said, pointing out the differences in her brush strokes and paint colors.

"Almost like you grew up a bit while I was gone," he whispered.

"Is that coming from Hunter the TA or Hunter the boyfriend?"

Amber tilted her head to gaze into those hypnotizing eyes, feeling herself falling into a spell.

"I think Hunter the TA just left town."

Hunter wrapped his arms around her. "But even in Paris, Hunter the boyfriend is always with you."

Chapter 25

The afternoon after Hunter returned to Paris, Amber painted in a frenzy. Techno pop thumped in the background. Two of her paintings rested against the wall while she added finishing touches to the final one. Immersing herself in her art helped soothe the emotional ache of Hunter's departure.

Amber stuck her brush in a jar of turpentine and headed to the bathroom to wash up. Soaping up her hands, she smiled at her image in the mirror. A blob of crimson paint dotted her left ear. Both cheeks were smudged yellow. Orange flecks splattered her jeans and tee shirt.

Her hands were impossible to clean properly. Dried paint rimmed her nails. She got the worst off and gave up. Her stomach rumbled, reminding her she hadn't eaten in hours. Without Hunter around, she often forgot to eat.

In the kitchen, she dug deep into the freezer and found a packaged dinner to pop in the microwave. While she waited, she checked her e-mail, expecting a notice from the Financial Aid Office about the following term. Scrolling down, she stared at one particular subject line.

She blinked twice to make sure she was reading correctly. Hello From Paris! But the e-mail, with an attached photo, was from Kayla. Delete it, she told herself. She's just trying to bait you. Biting her lip, Amber gave in to temptation and opened the file.

Kayla and her mother posed in front of the Eiffel Tower. Amber studied the photograph carefully, forcing herself not to be taken in. Kayla had lied before. There was nothing here to make Amber believe that anything had changed in her status with Hunter. For all she knew, this was an old holiday picture. Amber forced herself to close the file and push her laptop away.

She refused let Kayla's pathetic tricks get under her skin. Even if Kayla was in Paris, what was that to Amber? She had no evidence of the girl having any contact with Hunter. Kayla's family was grasping at straws to rattle her. It wouldn't work, Amber decided. Especially not after Hunter's incredible visit.

The microwave dinged and Amber shook her head. She needed to concentrate on getting this portfolio finished for class. Professor Collins had arranged for her class to meet at his house on New Year's Eve. In return for food, drink, and good cheer, he had asked students to bring their portfolios for short presentations. Allowed to bring a guest, Amber was grateful that Caleb, for once, was between his girlfriend of the week. He was happy to accompany her.

As Amber washed up her few dishes, her cell phone buzzed with a message.

Hannah: Hey Girl! John and I are in town tonight. Need to crash at your place for a week or so. Join us at Pete's Club around 11pm?

Amber stared at the message, furious. Hannah was clearly delusional. Or worse. She remembered her friend's glassy eyes and weird behavior Christmas Eve. Maybe Hannah was no longer merely experimenting with drugs.

Amber composed the message that was bound to end the friendship, such as it was. Instead of sadness, she only felt a surge of relief.

Amber: As I told you before, you cannot stay here. Cheap hotel called Willow Inn off Route 30. Student friendly.

She hit send and tossed the phone to the side. She wasn't going to spend one more moment thinking about Hannah or her boyfriend. Hopefully, Hannah would decide to party elsewhere or simply go to the hotel.

Relieved by her decision, Amber returned to work and painted for a few more hours. When she went to the kitchen to grab another soda, she checked her phone and heaved a sigh of relief. Hannah might be furious, but at least she hadn't bothered to text back.

A little after six o'clock, Amber cleaned herself up, tossed on some fresh jeans and a plain button-down shirt, and headed out to the Range Rover. She had promised to pick Caleb up from his mom's house. In return, Mrs. Hanson had promised a home cooked dinner before they left.

Caleb's mom lived in a small neighborhood with compact homes built in the 1950's. Her house, the same one that Caleb had grown up in, was dated but meticulously tidy. The eat-in kitchen was painted a cheery yellow with red, checkered curtains and matching tablecloth. The chairs were metal and vinyl. Amber felt like she had been transported back in time.

Mrs. Hanson was a great cook and an excellent storyteller. While the three ate huge plates of fried chicken, creamy mashed potatoes, freshly made biscuits with honey and butter, and sliced pickled beets, she spun outrageous tales of Caleb and Hunter growing up together.

"So there I was, banging on the door for them to let me in. That precocious Hunter insisted that they couldn't unlock the door unless I guaranteed that I wouldn't punish them."

Caleb held up his hands, grinning.

"Really, it was all Hunter's idea."

"They thought they had me, but they didn't know who they were dealing with."

Mrs. Hanson winked at Amber.

Caleb chuckled, nearly choking on his soda.

"When Hunter saw her crawling through the kitchen window, he nearly had a heart attack!"

Mrs. Hanson grinned as she pushed her plate away.

"I chased those boys halfway around the block."

Amber laughed and helped herself to another serving of pickled beets.

"What happened?"

Caleb grinned. "Hunter screamed like a little girl when mom grabbed us by our shirt collars."

Mrs. Hanson reached over and ruffled Caleb's hair.

"You were such adorable little monsters!"

"Aw, Mom!" Caleb protested, blushing. He stood up abruptly and began to clear the table.

Amber remembered her manners and stood.

"Let us get these for you before we leave."

"That's not necessary, dear." Mrs. Hanson pushed away from the table and started to stand.

Amber leaned over and grabbed her hands firmly.

"Oh, but it is," she said with a sly grin. "I want to hear more stories about the boys."

While Amber and Caleb washed, dried, and put away the dishes, Mrs. Hanson kept them entertained. Amber was still chuckling when she slid into the driver's seat of the Range Rover.

"What? I don't get to drive back," Caleb teased, sliding into the passenger seat.

He reached down suddenly. "Hey, your phone is down here."

He fished Hannah's phone from between his feet.

"Oh, thanks!"

Amber took a quick look, saw that she had a new text from Hannah, and dropped the phone into her purse. She wasn't going to let Hannah spoil her good mood.

Later, after Caleb left for a date, Amber finally remembered her phone. She pulled it out and frowned at the message.

Hannah: On our way. What is your address? Can't find a listing for Hunter Webb.

Knowing Hunter kept an unlisted address, Amber typed in the hotel address instead. Hannah would be furious when she realized what Amber had done. But Amber was sick of this whole situation. Had she always allowed Hannah to push her around?

Sighing, Amber changed her clothes and escaped to Hunter's room. She left her phone on the kitchen table. All she wanted to do right now was to lose herself in her painting.

But once she got back to Hunter's room, her heart was no longer in the painting. She stretched out on his bed where his scent was still so fresh. She knew he was already asleep in Paris. How in the world was she going to survive his absence?

Chapter 26

Amber painted most of the night and fell asleep, exhausted, in the wee hours of the morning. She didn't even hear Caleb come in. By the time she stumbled out to take a shower, he had already left for work. Having no plans other than painting, she had insisted he take the Range Rover for the day.

Amber avoided her phone until after she had scrambled herself some eggs and microwaved several strips of bacon. Finally, she reviewed her messages. She smiled at two new texts from Hunter. One asked if she was eating properly. She took a selfie with the bacon and eggs and sent that out first. Another message said that he would try to call her that evening. She sent back a quick message.

Amber: Can't wait!!!!!!

Amber ate her breakfast and tidied up the kitchen. Finally, she reluctantly checked Hannah's messages. The first had been sent the previous evening. Hannah had also tried to call. Amber's phone log showed twelve calls. But when she checked her voice mail, there were no messages. Amber felt a hard knot in her stomach as she scrolled through Hannah's texts.

Hannah: What the heck are you trying to pull?

Hannah: Took a cab to this stupid hotel thinking it was your place and now we are stranded!

Hannah: Come pick us up!

Hannah: Sweetie, this isn't funny anymore.

Hannah: I'm not kidding. We are really stranded here. John is a little low on cash.

Hannah: Amber?

Hannah: Amber?

Hannah: We won't be mad. Just come and get us.

Hannah: You are a crappy friend.

Hannah: Amber?

This message was around eleven o'clock the previous evening. However, the messages had picked up again around nine o'clock that morning. Amber glanced at the clock on the microwave. It was almost eleven now.

Hannah: Look, sorry if I sounded a little harsh. But I am really in a bind and could use a friend to help me out. Okay?

Hannah: We are still at the hotel. Pick us up and let's sit down and talk about what's going on with you.

Hannah: Okay, we have enough money for a cab ride to your place. Just give me the address.

Hannah: Amber?????

Hannah: Amber, send your address!!

Amber wanted to feel nothing but anger. She had to stay tough. Hannah had family she could depend on to help her. There was no need to allow Hunter, Caleb, and herself to be used.

Instead, she felt conflicted. Hannah's family had always been there for her. But this wasn't just Hannah. Who was this loser boyfriend? Amber had no inclination to even meet him, let alone cater to his needs. Finding her resolve, she typed in a reply.

Amber: I do not have the car today. Would you like me to call your Dad to get you?

She winced as she hit the send button, glad she wouldn't be able to hear Hannah's initial reaction.

Hannah: Where is the car? Call your roommate. Tell him to pick us up and bring us to the apartment.

Amber: Caleb is at work. Cannot pick you up.

Hannah: Give us Caleb's work address. Tell him we need to borrow car. Will return it by tomorrow morning.

Amber stared at the screen, stunned. So it was still all about the car? She stabbed in her response.

Amber: No!!

Tossing the phone to the side, she stood up, sniffling. She was angry and hurt. What was going on with Hannah? That was it. She no longer considered the girl her friend.

She stormed into Hunter's room and blasted the stereo. Gathering her best brushes, she grabbed a clean palette and squirted on smears of colors. Using her fingers, she mixed quickly, needing the solitude and solace that only her art could bring right now.

Two hours later, Amber felt spent. However, her final painting was now complete. She appraised it with a critical eye, making a few minor adjustments. Finally, she forced herself to stop. She knew that tampering with the painting at this stage would only ruin it. She still had to prepare a small write-up for each work, but otherwise she was ready for the presentation. She sighed, happy with the results. For the first time that week, she felt excited about the upcoming New Year's Eve Party at Professor Collins' house.

She walked into the kitchen, saw her phone, and grinned. She had nearly forgotten that Hunter was planning to call this afternoon. She calculated the time difference in her head. The gallery closed at nine o'clock this evening. So the earliest he could call would be three o'clock her time. Although he had a dinner break, the Lebas household was always too chaotic for a normal conversation. During the last attempt, Amber had gotten an earful of French from both four-year-old twins as they chased Hunter around the house.

Amber checked the clock. Two thirty. She still had at least half an hour. Most afternoons, she would have been at work. Even when she was available, Hunter usually was not. The Lebas family frequently entertained local artists, and it was part of Hunter's job to make sure that everyone was attended to. Unfortunately, the art world was not a nine-to-five job.

About ten minutes later, she heard a buzz alerting her to a text message.

Hunter: Hey, beautiful! Looking forward to our call. Can't wait to hear what you had for lunch.

Oops! She hadn't eaten since breakfast. Amber ran to the fridge and jerked it open. No leftovers. She opened the freezer. One lonely frozen dinner stuck in the back corner. That would have to do. She threw it in the microwave and slammed the door. While her food cooked, she sent a message.

Amber: Counting down the minutes.

Hunter: I bet you didn't eat lunch.

Amber: Why would you say that?

Hunter: I know you.

Amber: I had a late breakfast and now am having a late lunch.

Hunter: I knew it!

Amber: Don't you want to hear about my paintings?

Hunter: Later. Stop sending messages and eat.

Amber sighed and put the phone down. She knew he wouldn't send a single message until he thought she was finished eating. What a control freak!

Ten minutes later, she halfheartedly chewed a rubbery Salisbury steak. She had cooked the dinner a little too long. The peas were shriveled up, and the mashed potatoes tasted dry and unappealing. She swallowed what she could before dumping the rest in the garbage. She grabbed an apple to munch on.

Glancing at the clock, she saw she still had ten minutes before the gallery closed. She grabbed a magazine, wishing for once that they had a television set. She could use a mindless diversion.

Her phone buzzed again, and she snatched it up.

Hunter: Is the fridge stocked?

Ugh! What was it with his obsession with food? She was tempted to lie. But she knew that he would simply ask Caleb to verify.

Amber: Shopping right after my shift tomorrow.

Hunter: No food in the house? Very disappointed.

Amber: There is food. Nobody is going to starve.

Hunter: So show me what you will be having for dinner.

Amber: Don't you have work to do?

Hunter: No dinner? Do you have money for takeout?

Amber: The gallery is calling. They're looking for their intern.

Hunter: Are you making me worry about you on purpose?

Okay, that hurt a little. Amber grimaced. She knew that he was simply trying to help. But why couldn't he see that it drove her nuts when he was this controlling?

Amber: I'm sorry. I'll order takeout for dinner.

Hunter: Order Chinese from our favorite place. It will make me happy to know you are having a decent meal.

Amber: I like you happy.

Hunter: Me too! So promise?

Amber: Okay, okay, I promise.

A few minutes later her phone rang and Amber forgot to be annoyed at Hunter. The first sound of his voice made her melt. He told her about his latest adventures while she shared her more mundane world. Far too soon, though, he had to end the call.

"I've got to be up early for an appointment at the gallery," he explained.

"I understand," Amber said. And she did. But that didn't make her feel any better as they said their final goodbyes.

She hung up feeling even lonelier than before. Trudging to her bedroom, she sank onto the bed for a late afternoon pity cry for herself.

She drifted to sleep, dreaming of Hunter's beautiful green eyes.

<h1 style="text-align:center">Chapter 27</h1>

Amber woke to soft knocks on her door.

"Amber?" The voice belonged to Caleb.

She sat up. "Just a second!"

"Sorry if I woke you," Caleb said, rubbing the back of his neck as he headed for the kitchen.

"But Hunter sent me a text earlier today saying that you wanted Chinese for dinner. Asked me if I could make sure that you didn't forget to order it."

"Of course he did." Amber groaned. "Mr. Food Police figured out that we forgot to go food shopping."

Suddenly she had a disturbing thought.

"Hey, was he angry at you for the lack of groceries?"

Caleb didn't look at her. He turned and busied himself getting a soda.

"Um . . . He mentioned that we might want to pick up some things," he said vaguely.

He grabbed the takeout menu. "I'm starving. Do you mind if we go ahead and order now?"

He held up his phone. "I circled the things I wanted. Are you getting your usual or do you need to look at the menu first?"

Amber wanted to push the issue of Hunter. But she didn't want things with Caleb to be any more awkward.

"The usual," she said.

She still thought it was unfair for Hunter to take out his frustrations on Caleb. But Caleb was a big boy. He undoubtedly knew how to deal with his friend better than she did.

"Great! I'm going to work on a couple of assignments while we wait. Can you just let me know when the food gets here?"

"Sure, go ahead."

Amber pulled out her laptop. She might as well work on the descriptions of her art pieces while she waited. She was able to get the first two finished before she heard the delivery guy knocking on the door.

Getting up, she grabbed her purse so that she could pay. But when she offered the guy money, he simply smiled.

"It's okay, Miss. The food always goes on your account."

Amber blinked at him in confusion. "We have an account? Since when?"

"At least as long as I've worked here." The delivery guy smiled at her.

"Oh, well, here's a tip then," Amber said, giving him some cash.

"Thanks, Miss. Have a great evening!"

The delivery guy clattered down the stairs as Amber shut the door and carried the food inside.

"Caleb, food's here!" she called out and waited for him to come out of his room.

"Great! I'm famished!"

Caleb washed his hands in the sink and grabbed plates from the cabinet. When he saw Amber simply holding onto the bags of food, he looked startled.

"Is something wrong?"

"Did you know that the bills for the takeout go on an account?"

Caleb shrugged. "Sure. That's how Hunter set it up in the beginning. Why? Did they take your money?"

Amber studied him for a moment. "No, I only tipped him."

Caleb looked confused. "And you're upset why exactly?"

Amber sighed with exasperation.

"So what happens to the money that I've been contributing every time we order?"

"Oh, that! Hunter just has me . . ." Caleb broke off and looked alarmed.

Amber narrowed her eyes at him.

"Hunter has you do what exactly?"

Caleb swallowed nervously and then reached for the bags of food.

"No big deal. He just has me put it in the desk drawer."

Amber pulled the bags out of reach. "I thought that was where the bills went."

"Well, yes. Those too."

Caleb reached for the food again. "Seriously, Amber, you're making too much of a deal about this. I'm starving."

Amber shoved the bags of food across the table. She moved to the far corner of the living room where Hunter had an antique, roll-top desk tucked away.

"Where's the key?"

"Aw, Amber, you're killing me here! If Hunter finds out that I upset you, he's bound to take my head off."

"Well, that puts you in a bad spot, then. Because if you don't give me a key, I'm going to have a meltdown."

Caleb chuckled. "I'm sorry, Amber. But I'll take my chances with you."

Amber stormed over, furious.

"Although if looks could kill," he added quickly, "I'd definitely be avoiding you."

Amber kicked him in the shins, using the side of her foot as she'd been taught.

"Ow! There's no need to get violent!" Caleb hobbled away. "Okay, I was wrong! I'll deal with Hunter!"

Amber grabbed his arm, pulling him to the desk.

"The key?" she demanded.

Caleb pointed to a hidden nook.

"Between you and Hunter, I think I need a bodyguard," he muttered.

Amber unlocked the drawer and stared at the large pile of cash stacked neatly to one side of a pile of receipts. She didn't have to ask whether it was all her money. Of course it was. She slammed the drawer shut.

She stormed into the kitchen. She wanted to be mad at Caleb, but he looked like somebody had kicked him. Oh, yeah. She had actually kicked him. She winced. He really hadn't deserved that.

"Um . . . I'm sorry I kicked you," she said. "He just frustrates me to no end!"

She beat her fists on the table and Caleb jumped.

Amber giggled at his look of alarm. "I promise I won't kick you again."

Caleb backed away, rubbing his shin. "I'm not ever making you mad again."

Now Amber felt mortified. She couldn't believe she had lost control like that.

"Seriously, Caleb, I am so sorry! The guy who taught me that would furious if he knew."

Caleb appraised her, nodding his head thoughtfully.

"Does Hunter know about your ninja moves?"

Amber laughed. "No, I suppose not."

"So . . . You could say that you've been keeping something from him?"

"What? It's not like that. It's just never come up. I'm not trying to deceive him."

Caleb hesitated. "Um . . . You left your phone on the table last night."

Amber narrowed her eyes at him. "And?"

"And I swear I wasn't snooping. But the darn thing buzzed all night. I thought maybe Hunter was trying to get in touch with you. And . . . Well, I saw the messages from Hannah."

Amber swallowed.

"Yeah, well, she and I are having a huge argument right now."

Caleb looked torn. "I'd rather not be involved in your private life. But that was some pretty intense stuff. She was trying to get the address here."

He lowered his head. "I shouldn't have, but I scrolled up to see what was going on."

Amber glowered at him. "I can't believe you invaded my privacy like that!"

As soon as the words slipped out, Amber remembered how she had read Hunter's letter from Isabelle Lebas. Well, that was different. Wasn't it?

To her surprise, Caleb jerked his head back up, his face hard.

"And I can't believe that somebody was demanding that you steal Hunter's car and you didn't bother mentioning it! I saw my name on those texts. Don't you think I would like to know a little detail like that? You know, in case somebody tries to carjack me?"

Amber gaped at him.

"Look, I know Hannah sounds psychotic. But I have this situation under control. You don't need to worry."

Caleb stared at her in disbelief.

"So, you're vouching that this girl isn't planning anything bad for me or you? That she's just blowing off steam?"

Amber glared at him.

"I said I had things under control. Which is the whole point of this conversation. Somehow, you and Hunter are under the impression that I need to be babied."

"That's not fair!" Caleb's face darkened.

"Look, I know you think that Hunter was a jerk for not telling you about the takeout being on an account. But did you consider that maybe he did it on my behalf? And that he had to figure a way to accept your money without you feeling like your contribution meant nothing?"

"But only my money is in the drawer," Amber said. "Not yours."

"Because I have a prior arrangement with Hunter," Caleb said, his eyes dangerous.

"Which is?" Amber demanded. She immediately regretted asking.

She held a hand over her stupid mouth. What was wrong with her tonight? Everything she did and said was inappropriate.

Caleb looked hurt, but he stayed silent.

"I'm so sorry! That is totally none of my business, Caleb. I'm running off at the mouth and I should just shut up."

Caleb studied her for a minute. He took several deep breaths and slowly relaxed. Finally, he gave her a cautious grin.

"Does that mean I get to eat without getting beat up?"

"That can be arranged." Amber smiled, relieved to know that the tension between them was gone, at least for now.

She waited until Caleb had started eating before she asked what puzzled her the most.

"What was he going to do with the money?"

Caleb looked uncomfortable.

"Maybe you should ask Hunter." He shifted and then seemed to make a decision.

"If it makes you feel any better, Hunter doesn't make it a habit to talk about you with me. I know he can be controlling, but he would never do anything to hurt you."

Amber sighed and put her fork down.

"I know! I know! I must seem like a maniac. It's just that I've never been able to rely on anyone before. It's really hard when you've had only yourself to depend on."

Caleb held out a hand and touched her arm.

"Look, Amber, I get it. More than you can imagine. But you really have to figure out who your real friends are. You don't have to face all your problems alone. Let us help you."

Amber finished her meal in silence. Now that her anger was spent, she was surprised to discover how hungry she was. She looked up and saw that Caleb was watching her with a relieved look. He looked away quickly as though guilty.

"What?"

"Um . . . Nothing really."

Amber smiled sweetly. "Caleb, don't make me hurt you again."

"Aw, come on, Amber. Don't even joke about that anymore. My leg still hurts."

"Oh, don't be a baby! Let me see."

But when Caleb pulled up his pant leg, Amber gasped and put a hand over her mouth.

"Oh, Caleb! I feel terrible! That is going to be one nasty bruise."

Caleb winced. "Don't worry. I'll be fine. Just be available the next time I need a bodyguard."

Amber felt sick. "Seriously, Caleb, I've never intentionally hurt someone before. At least not anyone who didn't fully deserve it. You must think I'm a monster."

Caleb took her by the shoulders and looked her in the eyes.

"Look, Amber. I'm a big boy and I've been in a lot of big boy fights. I've broken a few bones and shattered a few noses. I've also taken my share of lumps."

He shook her shoulders lightly.

"Seriously, I'm fine. I should have never made the assumption that you were a weakling. That was one of my first lessons growing up. I'm embarrassed I let you get in that first shot."

He grinned and released her, heading for his room. Then he turned suddenly.

"If anyone asks, I whacked my leg on the coffee table. I'd never live this down at the gym."

Amber washed up the few dishes and put away the remaining takeout leftovers. She would leave Caleb a note asking for a grocery list. She could get the things after her shift ended.

She checked the time. Already after eight o'clock. If it wasn't after three in the morning in Paris, she would have been tempted to call Hunter. Instead, she finished her write-ups for art class and worked on her history notes.

As she climbed into bed, she started to think about what Caleb said about her keeping things from Hunter. Would he feel obligated to say something to Hunter? Ugh! Hunter would explode if he thought that she was keeping something important from him. But she had everything under control. There was no need to involve Hunter. Was there?

Sighing, Amber got out of bed, determined to make Caleb promise to keep the texts from Hannah a secret. But when she tiptoed to his door, his lights were already out. She padded back to bed. But now she was wide awake. She went to get her laptop, unable to control her curiosity any longer. Had Kayla sent another e-mail? She knew she shouldn't even be looking, especially when she had to get up so early the next morning.

There was another one. "Wish You Were Here!" Amber clicked the e-mail. Up popped another photograph. Clenching her teeth, she clicked open the file. This one was different. Kayla stood in front of a small café, holding a newspaper and pointing to something on it with one of her scarlet fingernails. Swallowing hard, Amber enlarged the photograph until she could see the date of the French paper, Le Monde. She had to translate the date using Google, but at last she had it.

Okay, that was weird. Christmas Day. Why had Kayla sent a picture of herself in Paris on Christmas Day? Suddenly, Amber grinned. If Kayla thought that sending her a photograph on Christmas Day from Paris was going to upset her, then she had no idea that Hunter had flown here. And if she didn't know that, then wasn't that clear evidence that she and her mother had no contact with them?

Yeah, you might have had a nice little dinner in a café, Amber thought smugly. But Hunter was here with me. Shoving aside her laptop, Amber crawled into her covers and snuggled with Hunter's pillow until she fell asleep.

Chapter 28

Amber woke up early the next morning because she was working a full day shift. When she finished showering, Caleb was already at the table eating a plate of French toast.

"Did I miss that in the freezer?" Amber asked, her mouth watering.

"Nope! I just made it. I made you some as well." Caleb grinned and motioned to the top of the stove.

"I found half a pint of cream and two eggs in the fridge."

Amber took the plate off the warmer and sat down next to Caleb.

"I thought all the bread was gone," she said, slathering the toast with butter and syrup.

"Fortunately for you, Hunter hates the end pieces from the loaves of bread. I won't let him throw them away and they get shoved to the back of the fridge."

Amber had a sudden inspiration.

"Wait, a second! Don't eat that last bite just yet."

Grabbing her phone, she scooted her own plate next to Caleb's and took a selfie highlighting the two of them with forks raised in front of the French toast.

"What's that all about?" Caleb asked. "Can I finish now?"

"Go ahead. I'm just sending proof to Hunter that we're not starving ourselves."

Caleb nodded appreciatively. "Good idea! By the way, I started on a grocery list. I'll finish it before I come by at five."

"Sounds good," Amber murmured.

She typed out her text to Hunter and attached the photo.

Amber: Newsflash – Caleb shows survival skills and produces bountiful breakfast!

After she finished brushing her teeth and grabbing her purse to head out the door, she noticed the return text from Hunter.

Hunter: Newsflash – Responsible roommates do not need to rely on survival skills.

Amber snarled at the phone. When it buzzed again, she almost didn't check.

Hunter: I dreamed about you all last night.

Amber softened. Ugh! She couldn't stay mad at him when he said stuff like that.

Amber: I miss you too.

Hunter: Have a great day at work!

Amber: You too!

Hunter: Are you in the car? I don't want you to be late.

Amber ran out the door and hurried down the steps. Caleb was already in the driver seat of the Range Rover when she slid in the passenger side. As soon as he backed out of the driveway, she texted Hunter back.

Amber: Caleb driving me now.

Hunter: Hmm . . . Took you almost two minutes to respond. I take it Caleb was waiting on you?

Amber: Don't ruin the good moment you had going.

Hunter: Sorry. I just know you so well.

Amber: I never said you were right.

Hunter: Ha! Ha! But you didn't deny it.

Amber: So I deny things?

Hunter: I'm going to stop before I get in trouble. I have a meeting in five minutes, anyway.

Amber: Goodbye then.

Hunter: Later, baby.

Caleb tapped on the wheel with his fingers as he waited for a traffic light.

"How's our friendly control freak this morning?"

Amber laughed. "In a remarkably good mood. Apparently, the photograph of French toast brought up good memories for him. He was actually warm and fuzzy."

Caleb chuckled. "If that's the case, I'll be making a lot more French toast in the future. A happy Hunter means a happy Caleb."

Amber hopped out of the car when Caleb pulled up to the loading zone in front of the store.

"See you this afternoon! Have fun at the camera shop."

Caleb waved as he drove off.

As she walked in, Amber realized she was actually early. Remembering that she hadn't had any food to pack a lunch, she walked to the deli section to have a sandwich made. She purchased a couple of bottles of water and a box of animal crackers to go with it. See, she wanted to tell Hunter. I can be responsible.

No one was in the break room. Amber laid out her purchases and took a photograph. She couldn't resist sending Hunter one more text message, even though she knew he was in a meeting and wouldn't be able to respond right away.

Amber: Humble, responsible roommate purchases lunch ahead of time.

She attached the photograph and hit send before putting everything back in the plastic bag and sticking it in the fridge. She used a store sticker to write her name and put it prominently on the bag. Anything unlabeled in the fridge was considered fair game for other employees.

Amber was stuffing her purse in her locker when she heard a buzz indicating she had a message. She swiftly pulled out her phone and grinned. Hunter had sent her a smiley face. That in itself was hilarious as Hunter wasn't a fan of emoticons. But she resisted the urge to text back. He should be paying attention to his meeting. And she was going to be late if she didn't leave the break room right now.

In the middle of the day, Amber found herself bored out of her mind. It was a slow afternoon and her particular register was at the far side of the main entrance. She was grateful when she got a small line of customers.

"Amber! Hi!"

Amber looked up with surprise to see Megan in her line. She gave her blue-eyed classmate a smile before helping bag the last bit of an elderly woman's order.

Finally it was Megan's turn and Amber rang up a huge pile of cheap noodles, a half gallon of milk, and a box of cereal.

"I didn't realize you were staying on campus during break," she said. "I would have had you over for dinner."

"I work most nights," Megan said, shrugging. She reached up to pull back a strand of coppery hair from her face.

"What about tonight? Are you free?" She quickly put Megan's purchases in a bag while her friend searched for the correct change.

Megan smiled and Amber noted again how pretty the girl was.

"Are you sure? Your roommate wouldn't mind?"

Amber smiled. "Not at all. Caleb's a nice guy. It would be fun."

"Should I bring anything?" Megan moved out of the way of the next customer.

"Nope. I'll call you a bit later with details about when we'll eat."

Amber waved at Megan and turned to her next customer. When she clocked out at the end of her shift, she found Caleb waiting outside the break room.

"Hey, I hope you don't mind, but I invited a classmate over for dinner."

Caleb grimaced. "Please tell me it's a girl. I don't want to risk a matching bruise on my other shin from the control freak."

"At least you would have matching legs," Amber teased. "But, seriously, it's a girl."

She took him by the shoulders. "But I'm warning you right now. She's not a candidate for girlfriend of the week club."

Caleb gaped at her. "Girlfriend of the week club?"

Oops! She hadn't meant to say it like that.

"Well, really, Caleb. What do you expect people to think? We never see a girl more than once or twice and then she gets replaced."

Caleb blushed. "It isn't like that. I mean . . . Okay, so maybe I have a hard time finding the right girl."

Amber smirked. "Out of all those girls, there hasn't been even one that met your strict qualifications?"

Caleb folded his arms across his chest. "Okay, I know I seem like a player but, honestly, most of these girls are the ones coming on to me."

"And, of course you can't disappoint them without bringing them home at least once," Amber said, her voice light.

Caleb bit his lip and sighed. "Look. I would love to have a great girl like you. Hunter really lucked out meeting you."

He shrugged. "You just don't understand. Some of those girls just want a good time. If the right girl ever comes along, then I'll change my evil ways."

Amber laughed.

"I'm not attacking you, Caleb. Most of those girls seem to be airheads."

She smiled and patted his shoulder. "But Megan is not an airhead. So behave yourself."

Caleb smiled. "I'm intrigued. What does she look like?"

Amber walked over and grabbed an abandoned empty cart.

"I'm warning you, Caleb. You hurt her and I'll hurt you."

"Point well taken." Caleb increased his stride to catch up with her.

"Do you want me to cook dinner tonight?"

Amber stopped and put her hands on her hips. She frowned.

"Are you saying I'm not a very good cook?"

"Did I say that?" Caleb winced. "Keep your little ninja feet on the ground. Your cooking is . . . um . . . okay."

Amber laughed. "I'm just kidding. I'd be the first to admit that I'm not the best cook in the world. I don't think I'm going to make a very domestic wife."

Caleb considered Amber a moment and shrugged his shoulders.

"Lucky for you, Hunter likes takeout. Actually, he can cook decently when he feels like it."

Amber pretended to be interested in a can of tomato sauce. This sudden talk about relationships and marriage, even if hypothetical, made her feel a bit weird. It brought up her encounter with Kayla. Who was she kidding? Could Hunter ever accept her with her past? For now, yes. But for marriage?

"So I was thinking that I could do a nice chicken braised in wine sauce," Caleb was saying beside her.

Amber forced herself to pay attention.

"Braised chicken in wine sauce? Sounds fabulous. Are you sure you're not trying to show off for Megan?"

"I don't even know what Megan looks like because little ninja doubts my integrity."

Amber laughed. "You'll see soon enough. What time shall I have her come over?"

Caleb checked the time on his phone.

"Have her come by at six thirty. We can get some appetizers together by then and I'll have the chicken ready for the oven."

Amber pushed the cart down the aisle.

"We'd better get a move on then. We still have a good bit to get for our regular shopping list."

Chapter 29

Once they returned home, Amber put away groceries while Caleb prepped for dinner. Amber watched in amazement as he quickly sliced onions, carrots, and peppers with precision. She knew he could make breakfast items like French toast. But she had never seen him put together a whole meal. Who would have thought that a boy with muscles like that would be so at home in the kitchen?

"Um . . . Did you spend time in a cooking school?"

Caleb looked up and grinned.

"Mom taught me when I was just a kid. I always helped out because she was so tired when she got home from work."

Amber smiled. "Your mom is really great."

She studied Caleb, seeing him in a new light. "You've been a really good son."

Caleb simply smiled back. "She did everything for me. I'll always look out for her."

"Well, I'll have to thank her for cultivating such a good chef. If I had known, I would have pestered you before now to make dinner."

Caleb laughed. "This isn't going to be a new thing, you know. I'll be back to my lazy ways soon enough."

Amber finished putting the last of the groceries away.

"So, what should I be doing in the way of appetizers?"

She smiled slyly. "This may be your one and only time to get to boss me around."

Caleb merely checked the time and pointed.

"There's a platter in that cabinet you can use for cheese and crackers. We'll keep it simple."

Amber got to work, slicing cheese, and arranging crackers on the platter. She found a nice bowl for the dark cluster of grapes Caleb had chosen. She put everything on the coffee table.

She was setting the table in the kitchen when there was a knock on the door.

"I'll get it," she said, seeing that Caleb was heating a pan over the gas burner.

"Hi, Megan!"

Amber gave her friend a hug. "I'm so glad you could make it tonight. Come on in."

"Wow. This is really nice!" Megan said, looking around in approval.

"Let me introduce you to Caleb before I show you around."

Caleb had added onions and carrots to the oil in the pan and they were now gently sizzling. He turned the pan on low heat and wiped his hands on the chef's apron he had tied around his waist.

"Megan, this is Caleb. Caleb this is my friend Megan. She's in my art and history classes."

Caleb and Megan exchanged pleasant greetings and Caleb returned to his cooking duties.

Amber took Megan into her room and was surprised when Megan softly pushed the door shut.

"Is something wrong?"

Megan giggled. "You didn't tell me your roommate was Caleb Hanson. Oh, my gosh. He's so hot."

Oh, no! Surely Megan wasn't going to fall for Caleb's charms.

"Okay, Megan, I have to tell you. Caleb is a great guy. He really is. But he has a revolving door of girls through here. I wonder if he has a commitment issue."

Megan winked. "Maybe he just needs the right woman."

Amber shook her head. She wasn't sure if this was a good thing.

Megan opened the door and raised her voice. "Such a cute room, Amber. I can see why you like it so much."

As they stepped into the kitchen, Caleb was pounding strips of chicken wrapped in plastic wrap. He pulled the wrap off and added it to the hot pan.

"This is awfully fancy for a student dinner," Megan said, watching Caleb work.

Caleb looked up and grinned. "I bet you were expecting spaghetti."

"Either that or macaroni and cheese." Megan sniffed the air. "Mm . . . This is going to be so much better."

"Do you cook at all?" Caleb asked.

"I love to cook," Megan said ruefully, pulling a chair to where she could watch Caleb work.

"But my budget calls for cheap noodles. There are only so many things you can do with those on a daily basis."

"There's an extra apron in that drawer behind you," Caleb said. "I'd love the help."

"Hey! I just asked you if you needed help," Amber said, her voice indignant.

Caleb leaned close to Megan's head and spoke in an exaggerated whisper.

"I let her slice the cheese and set the table. You might want to keep that in mind if she ever offers to cook for you."

Megan laughed, her blue eyes sparkling.

Watching them, Amber felt a sinking feeling. There was an electricity between the two that was undeniable. She just hoped that Megan wouldn't get hurt.

"Um . . . people? I can hear everything you're saying."

"Don't worry, Amber," Megan said, looking over her shoulder as she expertly peeled potatoes.

"Cooks love having people try out their dishes. You should take advantage of it."

Caleb moved closer to Megan. "Mashed? Or do you have a better suggestion?"

"How about potato cakes?" Megan suggested. "I haven't made them in awhile, but they should pair well with the braised chicken."

"Sounds good," Caleb murmured, staring down at her.

"How about a nice salad to go with it?" Amber asked, reminding them she was still in the same room.

"Even I can manage that."

"Actually, that would be perfect, Amber," Megan said, finally looking over. "Nice and light."

"A lime vinaigrette dressing with it?" Caleb suggested, waiting for Megan to turn around for approval.

"With a splash of honey for sweetness?" Megan responded, looking directly in Caleb's eyes.

Amber pushed between the two. "Okay, salad it is."

Once they sat down to eat, Caleb and Megan stared across the table at each other. For Amber's sake, at least the food was amazing.

"Seriously, you guys. How come I'm just now finding out how talented you two are in the kitchen?"

She might as well have been talking to herself. Answers to her questions were quick and in monotones. In the meantime, Megan started talking about how she loved graphic art.

"Really?" Caleb's eyes lit up. "I'm taking a course in that next semester."

When dinner was over, Megan excused herself to go to the bathroom.

Amber took the opportunity to speak to Caleb.

"Caleb, you promised!"

Caleb beamed at her. "Amber, this is it. She's the one!"

"Caleb, I know that she is very pretty. But I need you to remember our conversation about revolving girls."

Caleb shook his head. "You don't get it, Amber. My days of random dating are over."

Amber shook her head warningly. "I meant what I said about hurting her."

"Don't worry, ninja girl," Caleb said. "That's not going to happen."

"Ninja girl?" Megan asked curiously, coming up on Caleb and Amber so quietly that they both jumped.

Amber flushed, hoping Megan hadn't heard the conversation.

"Why don't you explain how you got the nickname?" Caleb asked wickedly. "I bet she would get a kick out of it."

"Do you really want me to explain?" Amber stared at Caleb defiantly.

Caleb stared back. "I suddenly don't care anymore."

Megan folded her arms and sat back down at the table.

"Well, this should be interesting! I'm not going anywhere until I hear all the juicy details."

"You can tell her or I can," Caleb said smugly. He took Megan's elbow.

"Why don't we go sit on the sofa? Amber and I'll get these dishes later."

Amber followed them over, hoping to sit between them. But Caleb blocked her with his legs and Megan was sitting on the end.

"Fine. I'll tell her." Amber turned to her friend.

"Last night I was upset with Hunter because he was showing some of his control freak tendencies."

Caleb watched expectantly, apparently enjoying seeing her squirm.

"I lost my temper and . . . um . . . kicked Caleb in the shin."

To her surprise, Megan laughed.

"Really, she kicked you? But she's so frail!"

She and Caleb shared giggles.

"I am not frail!" Amber shouted. "I'm as big as you are!"

Then she remembered the mark she left on his leg.

"Actually, I feel terrible about it," she said. "He's got a horrible bruise on his leg."

Megan looked from muscular Caleb to Amber as though in disbelief.

"It's really not that big of deal," Caleb said suddenly. "Honestly, I should have moved out of the way."

He laughed. "I just didn't realize that she had martial arts training. My error."

"No. Show her, Caleb," Amber insisted. "I was really a monster last night."

Caleb sighed. "Amber, seriously, that's not necessary."

"I still don't believe it," Megan said, crossing her arms. "You guys are playing games with me."

Caleb rolled up his pants. The bruise was turning a bluish-black color.

Megan put a hand to her lips. "You really did that?"

Amber sighed and nodded, feeling humiliated. She was stunned when Megan started to grin.

"Remind me to keep you around if I'm ever walking down a dark street by myself."

"Hey, where's the sympathy for me? I'm the one that nearly got crippled!" Caleb complained.

Megan laughed. "Oh, come on! A big, strapping fellow like you? You look like you'll survive."

Amber started to laugh. Megan's reaction was so totally different from what she had expected.

"Well, it's nice to know whose side you're on," Caleb teased, maneuvering even closer to Megan.

Amber narrowed her eyes at him.

"You know, I've told Caleb that anyone who hurts my friends will get bodily injured."

She smiled sweetly. "Of course, I'd have to inflict a little more damage than a simple bruise."

Megan surprised her by raising a hand. "Thanks, Amber, but I've got this one for now."

She turned to Caleb and put a hand on his knee.

"I like you, Caleb. But you should know that I'm very aware of your reputation with the ladies."

She shook her head gently when Caleb shot Amber an angry look.

"Don't be upset with her," she said. "She isn't the only one talking."

At that, Caleb actually looked shocked.

"I have a reputation on campus?"

Amber gaped at her friend. Megan seemed so much shyer in class.

"Some people think I'm a little too forthright," Megan said with a laugh. "The truth is that I just don't like games."

"Megan, I . . ." Caleb started to say.

Megan put up her hand again with a smile.

"Do you want to date me?" she asked Caleb outright.

Amber felt her mouth drop open.

Caleb's eyes widened, but he simply nodded.

"And I want to date you," she said calmly. "So this is what I need to happen."

Amber stared at Megan as though meeting her classmate for the first time.

"Number one," Megan said, lifting a finger.

"You and I will approach each other with pure friendship until you have proven yourself."

She lifted a second finger.

"Number two. You will immediately cease dating all other girls."

She lifted a third finger.

Amber noticed that Caleb was studying Megan with rapt attention. His eyes were shining as though he had just gotten the best gift in the world.

"Number three. If you can commit to keeping yourself pure for me for one month, then I will consider moving our relationship forward."

"Number four. If you fail in any of these steps, we may continue our friendship, at my sole discretion."

She placed her hand on her lap.

"Any questions?"

Caleb slowly shook his head.

"Are we in agreement?"

Caleb nodded as though in a trance.

"Excellent!" Megan stood suddenly. "Well, it has been a lovely evening, but I need my rest. I have a long shift tomorrow."

She turned and hugged Amber. "Thanks again for inviting me. I had so much fun. You're bringing Caleb to the party at Professor Collins' house, correct?"

Amber found her voice. "Yes. We'll definitely be there. Caleb's driving."

"Excellent!" Megan turned and shook Caleb's hand solemnly.

"Caleb, it has been a pleasure meeting you. I hope for both our sakes that you are able to meet my demands."

She leaned up and gently kissed his cheek.

"Also, you are a marvelous cook. I definitely want to do that again whether we are dating or just friends."

With that, she collected her purse and jacket and let herself out the door.

Amber stood gaping after her.

"I'm not sure what just happened. She's such a shy little thing in class!"

Caleb shook his head. He headed to the table and cleared the dishes as though in a daze.

"Amber, you are the most incredible person in the world for bringing Megan over tonight. I think I'm in love!"

Amber simply smiled and shook her head. They cleaned the kitchen quickly and then she headed to her room. In spite of her best intentions, she found herself drawn to the laptop. She had a feeling that Kayla was planning on sending another photograph. Did she have any way of telling if and when Amber opened the others? Or was she simply counting on Amber to be curious?

If Amber told Caleb about the photographs, Kayla could honestly say that they were innocent pictures. The photographs themselves were not provocative. In some ways, Amber had to admit it was rather ingenious. Kayla could torment her freely while looking like a nice fellow student sharing holiday memories.

Scrolling through her e-mail, she found another one from Kayla, just as she had expected. She didn't even pause this time before she opened it. At first glance, this photograph made her flinch. There was Kayla, standing in front of Hunter's art gallery! Amber felt her pulse quickening, but then looked closer.

Why stand outside the gallery if she was visiting Hunter? She zoomed in on the photograph and started to smile. There on the door was a sign. Fermé. She had to look it up to be sure but . . . Yes! The gallery was closed. Whatever game Kayla was playing, she was trying to keep it from Hunter.

Amber closed her laptop and stared off into space. Should this be something she should tell Hunter about? Nothing had actually happened. She sighed. Telling him would just stress him out. Even if he said something to Kayla directly, she could deny it. Also, how would she explain having heard Kayla and her mother's conversation?

She couldn't picture explaining to Hunter, or anyone else for that matter, how she ended up overhearing a private conversation while wedged behind a candy vending machine. No, she thought firmly. She would have to deal with Kayla and her mother on her own.

Chapter 30

Amber was up before six o'clock the morning of New Year's Eve. She took a quick shower to wake herself up. She had agreed to take the earliest shift at work today so that another student employee could travel home to be with her family. Amber's art project was complete and she could always use the extra cash. She was in the kitchen making breakfast when Caleb stumbled into the kitchen.

"I'm sorry. Did I wake you?" Amber asked. "I was trying to be quiet."

Caleb shook his head and yawned. His hair stuck up all over his head and he wiped sleepy seeds from his eyes.

"I thought I'd go out and take some photographs in the park this morning."

"Wow. I figured you'd be sleeping in. Does that mean you want to drive me to work so you can have the car?"

Caleb flushed. "Um . . . Actually, Megan is picking me up after breakfast."

Amber grinned. "Is that so? Was it your idea or hers to get up so early?"

Caleb groaned. "Hers. Apparently, she likes to get a fresh start on the day."

Amber giggled. "Huh! Well, maybe you really are in love. I can't remember the last time you were up this early without having a morning class or work."

"Mind if I throw a couple more eggs in if you're making scrambled eggs?" Caleb asked.

"I don't know," Amber teased. "Remember I'm a really horrible cook."

Caleb yawned again.

"Hard to mess up scrambled eggs," he said "But on second thought, why don't I do that for you."

Amber laughed. If being a bad cook meant that somebody always offered to take over for her, she could live with that.

"I'll be wanting toast and bacon too," she said. "I'll set the table and pour us some orange juice."

Amber had just finished her last bit of eggs when she realized that Caleb was watching her.

"What?"

"I don't want you to get upset," he started out, rubbing his neck. "But I just wondered if you had any more crazy texts from Hannah."

Amber dropped her fork on her plate with a clatter and stood up abruptly.

"I said I had things under control. But, no. There have been no new texts."

Caleb stood as well and cleared his dishes.

"Aw, come off it, Amber. You can't blame me for being a little worried. Your friend sounds like she's in some deep trouble. You don't know what somebody that desperate would do if they felt their back was against the wall."

"I think I know Hannah better than that," Amber said, dumping her dishes in the sink.

"I hope you do," Caleb muttered, heading off to his room.

Amber bit her lip. Hannah was saying some crazy stuff, but she wouldn't actually do anything dangerous. She wasn't that messed up. Was she?

Before she left for work, Amber double checked that her paintings were safely propped against the wall in Hunter's room. She had carefully wrapped each canvas in brown paper to prevent damage on the way to the party. She had placed her written notes in a clear binder. After checking to make sure she hadn't missed anything, she sent Hunter a quick text.

Amber: Off to work. Have a great day! Text me tonight when you get a chance.

She grabbed the keys for the Range Rover and opened the closet for a warm jacket. She sighed as she saw her lovely new boots there. Too bad they were impractical for being on her feet all day. Hmm . . . That didn't mean that she couldn't at least enjoy them on the way. Smiling, she kicked off her sneakers. The plush liner was soft and warm on her chilly toes. She threw the sneakers in a canvas bag and hurried out to the car.

Ugh! There was a thin sheet of ice on the windshield. She dropped her canvas bag on the ground and jammed her freezing fingers under her armpits. Did she have time to go and search for gloves? She sighed. Probably not.

She opened the driver's door, tossed her purse inside, turned on the engine and clicked on the seat warmer. She fished under the passenger seat for the ice scraper. Then, reluctantly, she slid out and attacked the window with the scraper. She worked as quickly as she could and then scrambled back into the car, shivering. Her fingers were so cold that they stung.

The seat warmer was a lifesaver. She sat on her fingers and sighed as the warmth spread through her hands. Checking the car clock, she found that she was making good time. The freezing temperatures had only made it seem like she had been scraping the windshield for longer than five minutes. Backing out of the driveway, she turned down the street. The streets were nearly empty this early in the morning.

As she drove, she thought about Hunter. Spending New Year's Eve apart was disappointing. At least working all day today might help keep her from dwelling on his absence. The party at Professor Collins' house would help fill part of the void. But that didn't start until seven.

She couldn't believe that she still had another full month to go without him. Even with the extra shifts at the store, she ached for him. Worse, every day apart made her doubt the future of their relationship. What would happen if Kayla or her parents tried to influence Hunter's parents against her?

Did Hunter's parents even know about her? She had been afraid to ask Hunter. She was worried that he would wonder why she wanted to meet them at this stage of their relationship. And if they did know, then she was afraid that they wouldn't want to meet her because of her past.

Pulling into the mostly empty parking lot, Amber found a spot to park and hurried out. To her surprise, she was actually early. She had to wait a few moments until another employee could let her in.

In the break room, Stacey was putting out coffee and donuts.

"Help yourself," she said, smiling. "Thanks for showing up on time."

Amber started to stow her jacket and purse in a locker when she heard the buzz of her phone. Oh, Hunter must be returning her text! She pulled the phone out, anxious to see his greeting.

Ugh! Not Hannah again! She started to throw the phone back in, but curiosity got the best of her. She might as well know what her ex friend was up to.

Hannah: Hey Girl! You are certainly hard to track down. Remembered you mentioned that you were working at the grocery store.

Amber groaned. So now Hannah knew how to find her. Her phone buzzed again.

Hannah: On my way back to mom and dad's house. Could you at least say goodbye before I leave?

Amber stared at the phone, perplexed. Hannah was still in town?

Hannah: I'm outside by your car.

Amber: Where's John?

Hannah: Oh, he left last night. I'm by myself.

Amber glanced at the clock. She had arrived so early that she still had ten minutes before her shift officially started. There couldn't be any harm in simply talking for a few moments. She would be firm, though, and insist that Hannah get some help.

Sonia, the romance reader, was the only other employee in the break room. Amber turned to her to leave a message.

"Hi, Sonia. A friend of mine is outside and wants to say goodbye before she leaves town. Can you let Stacey know I'll be back in a couple minutes?"

Sonia looked up from her novel.

"Sure, honey," she said, taking a bite out of a chocolate glazed doughnut.

Amber swung her purse over her shoulder, not even pausing to grab her jacket. She would only be outside for a few minutes.

The cold air whipped against her as she hurried from the store. Her bare fingers stung. Amber realized she still had the phone in her hands. Stopping by the door, she fumbled with her purse, trying to unzip it. The zipper caught on something and wouldn't budge. She reached for a back pocket and remembered she was wearing plain slacks. Ugh! Her fingers were freezing. She was stupid not to have brought the jacket.

She motioned to an employee and stepped back into the store. But when she saw the clock on the wall, she realized she had already wasted precious minutes. She didn't have time to get the jacket. At least her feet were warm. She stared down at the boots which came almost to her knees. Her thin legs allowed just enough room to slip the phone inside. Now she could at least tuck her hands under her arms.

Straightening up, she hurried outside once more. There were still only a few cars in the parking lot. Halfway to the Range Rover, she still didn't see Hannah. There was only one other car next to hers and she was certain that it belonged to another store employee. That was weird. Now that she thought about it, how had Hannah gotten here? How was she getting home? She stopped in her tracks, suddenly uncertain.

"Amber, over here!"

Hannah stepped from around the Range Rover, bent over and huddling against the cold.

"I got dropped off by the taxi and was trying to stay out of the wind," she called out.

Ugh! Not another plea for the Range Rover! This was going to stop right now. She would get Hannah inside before calling Frank. He could come and deal with his daughter.

"Hannah, come inside the store! It's freezing out here."

Hannah acted as though she couldn't hear her. She stepped back around the Range Rover. That girl could be so infuriating. Amber hurried over, her only thought to get Hannah and go back inside.

"Come on, Hannah! I'm not giving you the car!"

Amber walked around the Range Rover and then stopped, frozen in place, as she saw a gun pointed straight at her chest.

Chapter 31

Frank's self defense training never included what to do when staring down the barrel of a gun. At first, Amber could only think that she was about to die. Her vision was so focused on the gun itself that it took her several moments to take in the attached hand.

She followed the hand to the arm and then to the creep pointing it at her. His head was shaved, but there was enough growth coming back to show that he was going bald. Regular jeans, hiking boots, and a plain blue jacket. He didn't look particularly noteworthy. Except for the gun.

Amber's second thought was that her friend was also in grave danger. But Hannah, safe and sound, placed a hand on the man's shoulder.

"John, stop pointing that gun at her. I'm sure she's going to do what we say."

John? This creep was Hannah's boyfriend?

"Get her purse," John said.

He looked around nervously, waving the gun when Hannah didn't move.

"Get the purse or I swear I'll shoot her right here in the parking lot!"

Hannah walked over, her eyes glazed. Heavy bags sagged under her eyes. Her hair was matted and oily. When she reached for Amber's purse, her hands shook.

"Don't mind grumpy over there," she said, her feet unsteady. "As soon as we get some money, everything will be fine."

Amber let the purse drop from her shoulder. It was hard to move her arm because her muscles had all stiffened. John still had the gun pointed in her direction.

"Hannah?" Amber managed to whisper.

Hannah started crying. "It's all your fault! Why couldn't you just do what he asked from the very beginning?"

"Hannah, get back over here!" John started waving the gun again.

Hannah raced back and Amber found her voice.

"Just take the purse and the car," she said, her voice shaky. "There's enough cash for gas money."

"Shut up!" John yelled. "And start walking this way."

Amber wanted to turn and run. But John looked serious about shooting her. She shuffled forward, feeling like she was going to pass out. She was breathing hard and shaking from head to toe.

Hannah fumbled with the broken zipper on the purse. Finally, John reached into his pocket with his free hand and pulled out a knife.

"Hold the gun on her," he told Hannah.

Hannah's eyes widened, but she did as he told her. The gun wobbled in her hands.

"If she moves, pull the trigger," John said.

"But I can't shoot –"

John cut her off with a growl.

"If you don't, I'll kill both of you," he muttered, slicing open the purse so that the contents fell onto the asphalt.

The vials of Amber's glucose pills rolled on the ground. One disappeared beneath the Range Rover.

John ignored everything except the wallet and keys. He left the ruined purse on the ground.

"Where's the phone?" He grabbed the gun from Hannah and pointed it at Amber's chest.

"I . . . um . . . I think I left it inside. I was in a hurry. I forgot my jacket, too."

Amber's teeth chattered so hard that she wasn't sure John understood her.

But he simply looked around the parking lot quickly before opening the door to the Range Rover.

"Get in and don't do anything stupid. I would just as soon shoot you than drive your privileged self around."

Amber hurried over, her eyes on the gun, and tripped over the purse strap. She landed heavily on her knees and cried out.

"Get up!" John yelled above her.

Amber reached out to steady herself and her fingers touched a vial. Without even thinking, she grabbed it and stumbled to the car door, desperately hoping that a customer or employee would drive by and see them.

John flicked the gun in the direction of her stomach and Amber clambered in the back seat. As she started to sit, she remembered the vial of glucose pills in her hands. She hurriedly tucked it in her back waistband. Within seconds, both John and Hannah had climbed in as well. The sounds of the doors slamming shut made Amber jump.

Amber thought about screaming. But who would hear her? The parking lot was virtually empty. Unless Sonia got suspicious in the next few minutes, nobody would even know what had happened to her. The only positive thing was the phone hidden in her boot.

"Hannah, drive out to the cabin."

Amber's eyes widened. Cabin? What cabin? What were they planning to do with her? Now that they were out of the wind, she could feel nervous sweat pooling beneath her arms. Did Hannah have any control over John? Or was she too hopped up on drugs?

If John hadn't had the gun, then perhaps Amber could have tried to tackle him. But all the martial arts in the world couldn't stop a bullet. She thought of the stupid vial in her waistband. Why had even grabbed it?

As they headed away from the grocery store, John started to relax. He put the gun on his thigh, his finger just beside the trigger. Amber had to tell herself not to do anything stupid. Even if she managed to get in one good kick, she could be dead before Hannah even stopped the car. No, she would have to sit here and hope an opportunity presented itself.

She tried to follow where they were going but every time she tried to look out the window, John casually raised the gun and pointed it at her. She settled for staring at her lap and trying to count the seconds, hoping to at least keep track of how far they traveled.

And then her leg began to buzz. Someone was texting her. She tried to cough to mask the sound, but it buzzed a second time.

John laughed.

"Hand it over," he said. "Though I suppose I can't blame you for trying to keep it hidden."

Hands shaking, Amber fished the phone out of her boot. John grabbed it before she could see who had tried to text her. Opening the window, he flung the phone far into the woods.

"Don't want anyone to try to track you down with GPS."

Amber sank back against the seat. The phone had been her one hope of escape. After an agonizingly long ride, she felt the car leave the main road and start lurching down a bumpy path.

The gun jerked up off John's thigh, startling both him and Amber.

"Easy up there!" he yelled, not bothering to turn his head.

"This isn't even a road!" Hannah shouted back. "I hate this place! It's in the middle of nowhere and . . ."

"Shut up!" yelled John. "I'm sick of all your whining."

The front of the car went silent.

Well, that was a bad sign, Amber thought morosely. Nobody ever intimidated Hannah. Of course, none of her adversaries in the past had included criminals with guns.

Finally, the car lurched to a stop. John stood up and opened the side door.

"Out!" he commanded, waving the gun.

Amber climbed down, her legs shaking so badly she could barely stand. Was this it? Was he going to shoot her here and abandon her body?

"Stay in the car, Hannah!"

John turned to Amber and smiled. "I bet you're wondering if there are any bullets in here?"

Amber shook her head, unable to speak.

John pointed the gun at her head and put his finger on the trigger.

Amber moaned and squeezed her eyes shut.

She heard the gun go off and screamed. She opened her eyes, staring down in horror, wondering if and where she had been shot.

John laughed.

Hannah came running, her face ashen. "You said you wouldn't hurt her!"

"I didn't shoot her," John said calmly, smiling at them insanely.

"But if you don't get in the car, I'm going to shoot you." He swung the gun at Hannah's head briefly before turning it back in Amber's direction.

Amber felt dizzy with relief. She was still alive. But she wasn't sure for how long. John was clearly insane.

"I just wanted to show you how serious I am," John said smoothly. "Now, we're going to walk back here to this little shed. No funny business or I shoot for real."

Amber nodded numbly. She stumbled toward a derelict wooden shack. Further down the road, she could see a small cabin to the side.

"Eyes ahead!" John yelled and Amber turned to face the shed again.

When she reached the door, John opened it and shoved her inside. She fell on her knees, landing on a rusty shovel. Behind her, the door slammed, and she heard a clanking sound.

"Now, Hannah and I are going to go to a nice hotel and get cleaned up. If all goes well, then we send directions to where you are. If not . . . Well, you just better hope that your rich boyfriend wants you back enough."

John laughed. "Either that or you really like the sounds of nature."

She heard John's retreating steps as he walked back to the car. Moments later the Range Rover's engine started. The wheels crunched in gravel. And then there was silence. Amber was alone.

At first, she was terrified that John was simply playing a trick on her. Had he pretended to get in the car? Did he want her to walk out so that he could shoot her? Or would both of them be waiting at the end of the road?

Eventually, her aching knees forced her to act. She stood uneasily, trying to get her bearings. Although the shed had no windows, the warped boards allowed in chinks of light. She fingered the rusting tools, realizing that the roof must leak. Beneath her feet was only hard, packed earth. Straining to hear sounds of an engine, she peeked cautiously through a crack in the wall. She couldn't see any movement from the cabin about thirty feet away.

Was John working alone? Was someone waiting to shoot her if she came out? She swallowed down her panic.

She stood cautiously and pushed against the door. It wouldn't budge. She tried again, this time putting all her weight against it. She heard metal clanking and realized with a growing sense of horror that she was locked inside.

Chapter 32

She panicked at first, beating at the door until her fists were bruised and numb. She sat down, partially in shock. No wonder John and Hannah had simply driven away. She shivered, remembering the look of glee in John's eyes after he had fired the gun. Even if Hunter paid a ransom, she feared that John planned for her to die out here.

When would anyone even start to look for her? Would Sonia assume that she had skipped out on her shift? Even Caleb and Megan weren't expecting to see her until the end of her shift at three o'clock.

The cold seeped into Amber's thin slacks. She shivered uncontrollably. She stood and wiped her face with a dirty hand. *Don't panic. Get your heart pumping.* She jumped up and down, forcing her heart to beat harder. When she was breathless, she stopped.

You could be worse off, she thought. John could have shot you before he left. She looked down at her boots. The expensive leather and soft wool were keeping her feet and lower legs warm. She was lucky that she had given in to the temptation to wear them this morning.

But her fingers stung in the cold. How long would she last in this weather with no jacket, hat, or gloves? *Focus, Amber!* She squinted at the shovel she had tripped over.

Hmm . . . This was a tool shed. She started to sort through the tools, looking for anything sharp. Maybe she would get lucky and find an ax to chop her way out. No such luck. She discovered a rake, an old-fashioned push mower, a rusty bicycle with flat tires, and a wheelbarrow.

What else? A giant box of canning jars. Gardening gloves. Hey! She could wear those. Grabbing them, she stuffed her stiff fingers through. Not very warm but better than nothing. Then she spotted a wash tub with an old pair of rubber gloves and a scrub brush. Amber stared at the rubber gloves. Rubber was insulating right? If she wore them beneath the gardening gloves, her fingers should be much warmer. As a bonus, the rubber gloves came up to her elbows.

She kept searching, hoping to find something for her head. She poked behind the cardboard box of canning jars and found another set of gardening gloves. Now, if she could just find some sort of string. Wait. Was that a fishing pole hanging on a hook above her head? Yes!

Even jumping, she couldn't reach it. Ugh! Why did she have to be so short? She looked around, trying to find something sturdy enough to step on. She eyed several bags of soil. Those might work if she could pull them over. Or would the box of canning jars hold her? She lugged the box out of the corner. The box wasn't completely full, so the jars rattled around. She needed something flat for the top to distribute her weight.

She looked around in despair. There had to be something. The fishing pole was hanging from a hook. But could there be shelves as well? She squinted at the back wall behind the wheelbarrow and found one. Was it attached to the wall or simply loose? She carefully squeezed past the wheel barrow, grunting as she maneuvered her butt past the heavy bags of potting soil. She reached her hands up, stood on her tiptoes, and pushed with her gloved fingers.

The board moved and several Terracotta pots came flying down. One cracked her in the forehead and she cried out. But she kept her grip on the board and wiggled it toward her. Finally it slipped free and fell down, one corner banging her shoulder.

"Ouch!"

The board clattered to the ground. Groaning in pain, Amber sat down. Peeling off the gloves, she explored her head and felt something sticky. Blood. She pressed one of the gardening gloves hard against her forehead. Several minutes later, she pulled away the glove and gingerly touched her forehead. The cut stung, but it wasn't oozing any more. Her fingers, though, were stiffening in the cold. She put the rubber gloves back on and then stuffed her hands back into the large gardening gloves.

Same plan. Keep focused.

Crawling on her hands and knees, Amber retrieved the fallen shelf and slid it over the top of the box of canning jars. She had to get that fishing pole. Moving slowly to keep the dizziness at bay, she cautiously stood on the board and reached upwards. She had a moment of vertigo, but her fingers almost immediately found the fishing rod. She grabbed it and sank back down quickly.

She remembered seeing hedge clippers in the corner. She got to her knees and crawled there. After reeling out a large amount of fishing line, she was able to clip the ends and make her makeshift hat. She used several pieces of line to secure it to her head, making a final knot beneath her chin.

What else could she do? The ground was so cold! If only she had something like a tarp sit on. She looked around, finally thinking of the plastic bags holding the potting soil. As she pushed the box of canning jars out of the way, she considered the cardboard box. Cardboard was a good insulator as well.

When she flattened the box out, she was thrilled to see that she could curl up on it. It wasn't much. But at this point she would try anything to avoid freezing to death. She crawled over to the bags of potting soil, dragging the clippers behind her. Her blood sugar was dropping. If only she had some of those stupid glucose pills, she thought. And then she stopped, feeling along her back waistband. They were gone!

Starting in one corner, she searched the cold, packed ground. She crawled a few inches at a times, making large sweeping motions with her hands and arms. Finally, right by the door, she saw that the precious vial had rolled off to the side. With shaking hands, she fumbled with the cap. The pills spilled on the floor and she fought to pick them back up with the thick gloves.

Finally, she got one of the large, orange tablets into her mouth. As the glucose melted on her tongue, she groaned with relief. If she ever saw Hunter again, she was going to tell him that he was the most brilliant person in the history of the world. She ate two more before carefully scooping the rest back into the container.

Energized, she sliced the end of the potting soil bag and quickly scooped out huge piles of dirt. Finally, she was able to drag the partially empty bag off the wheelbarrow and dump out the remaining soil. Clutching her prize in one hand, she slowly crawled back to the cardboard mat as she shoved the clippers ahead of her. She sat on the cardboard and rested.

After some consideration, she shook out another glucose pill onto her dirty gloves. She popped it into her mouth, not caring that she got some potting soil in her mouth in the process. She closed her eyes, willing more strength to return. Using the clippers, she cut out a coarse plastic dress. When she was finished, she slipped the bag over her head. She smoothed the plastic dress over her body, getting to her knees so that her thighs were covered as well.

She wanted to curl up on the mat and simply sleep. Her ridiculous hat had shifted, and she reached up to straighten it. The edge of the gardening glove was uncomfortable against her cheek and the fishing line bit into her neck. But that was a small price to pay if it helped keep her from freezing to death. She forced herself to crawl back for the second plastic bag.

After emptying the second bag, she noticed how much warmer the soil was than the frozen ground. She shoved a thick layer in a pile and then put her flattened cardboard on top. She then stepped into the second empty potting soil bag. This was one time it paid to be short, she thought, as the bag reached her waist. Finally, leaning forward, she scooped piles of soil on top of the plastic to increase insulation. As she worked, her breath steamed in front of her face.

Finally, her energy flagging, she rested on the cardboard mat. With the second bag now covering her legs, she could allow herself the luxury of shifting the bag on her upper torso a bit higher. She adjusted the bag so that only her eyes, nose, and mouth remained uncovered. The top of her head and ears were now shielded in plastic. Her only fear was smothering. At the moment, however, that seemed like the least of her worries.

She tried to close her eyes and sleep. But the lumpy dirt beneath her hadn't made the earthen floor any more comfortable. She ached all over. For the first time, her mind was somewhat clear. She thought of Hunter and his amazing emerald eyes.

Had she ever told him how incredible he was? He called her gorgeous and baby all the time. But she had felt uncomfortable giving him affectionate nicknames. Why? Had she always just assumed that this relationship was temporary?

Was she keeping an invisible wall between herself and Hunter? Had he seen that? Was that why he had never mentioned the "L" word? Was that why she refused to use the word herself? Ugh! She was so messed up! Lying here, on the verge of potential death, she started to think about how precious life was. If she ever saw Hunter again, she was going to tell him how she really felt. Did she really love him?

Yes, she realized. Hunter was the one she wanted to spend the rest of her life with. And if she lived through this experience, she could deal with anything Kayla and her crazy mother threw her way.

Lying there in the dim moonlight, Amber imagined that Hunter was here with her, holding her in his arms. Warm arms. His chest would be radiating heat. He would look at her with those hypnotic green eyes and she would forget about how hungry and thirsty she was. She would forget about the cold and the way her body ached. She would only float in those eyes as though they were a sea of calmness. Breathe, he told her.

Breathe in. Fill your belly. Exhale, let your anxieties go. Breathe in. Breathe out. Sleep.

Amber woke to the sound of an engine. She sat up, panicking. Was John coming back to finish her off? She should try to find a weapon. Instead, she found herself paralyzed with fear. She tried to cry out, but her voice wasn't working.

The approaching engine got closer. Amber squeezed her eyes shut and curled into a tight ball as though she could make herself invisible. Surely, Hannah wouldn't let John kill her. Or had John killed Hannah? Amber's heart raced, and she started to sob. She did not want to die like this!

Chapter 33

Every creak in the old shack sent tremors of fear through Amber Holloway's body. Constant terror and numbing cold had left her exhausted. Part of her brain still couldn't accept that she was here.

But the nightmare wasn't over. Curled into a fetal position, all she could think about was how she wasn't ready to die.

Her brain played the sick footage of the day. Calling out for Hannah. Finding a gun pointed at her. The long ride to this remote location with her captor's gun always in view. John pointing the gun at her head and firing. His laughter at her terror.

And the cold. The cold that even now seeped into her bones in spite of the plastic bags and potting soil she had piled on top of herself. She didn't want to die like this.

Car doors slammed. Running feet pounded in the distance. Confused shouting.

When she dared to open her eyes, she saw bright lights flickering around in all directions. Somebody banged on the shed door.

She flinched, curling herself into a tighter ball.

"It's locked!" a voice called out.

More running feet. More voices approaching. Something heavy ramming the door. The old wood whined and creaked.

Amber moaned. She wriggled on the frozen ground, trying to escape into the shadows.

A hole appeared in the door. Gloved hands ripped off jagged strips of splintered wood.

Amber squeezed her eyes. Please don't let him kill me.

Hands moved across her body. Pawed at the dirt she had piled over her plastic blanket.

"She's here!" The voice was hoarse. Frantic.

In her delusional state, Amber thought it sounded like Hunter. But that couldn't be. Hunter was in Paris.

"Amber, it's me!"

Hunter? Amber opened her eyes. Found his face inches from her own. If she had any doubt at all, it was erased by the sight of those beautiful emerald eyes.

"Why are you crying?" Her tongue felt thick in her mouth. Her voice was a croak.

"Don't talk, Amber. Everything is going to be okay."

She stared at him, confused. Then remembered her captor. Nobody was safe.

"He has a gun. John has a gun, and he has Hannah."

"He is never going to hurt you," Hunter's voice was hard as steel. "They got him. He's in jail. You're safe."

She felt him slip the makeshift hat away from her head.

"This will be much warmer." He pulled his own woolen cap off and pulled it gently over her head and ears.

"Sir, we should get her to the hospital," a voice said.

Bright lights blinded her. She moved her head away and squinted.

"We're putting you in an ambulance, okay?"

Hunter scooped her up and she let her head loll against his chest.

Everything seemed unreal. A blur of faces. Uniforms. Steam puffing in the frigid air as people spoke. Gave orders.

Hunter laid her on the stretcher and two medics secured her with straps. She saw the night sky, clear with billions of stars. How pretty.

Then she was lifted up. There was a small bump as she was slid into the ambulance. The night sky was replaced with machines and a bright light shining above her head.

"I'm right here, baby." Hunter squeezed her hand.

The back of the ambulance door slammed shut.

A medic used scissors to clip away the plastic bag that had kept her from freezing.

She felt clots of potting soil trickle down the back of her neck. Lights were shined in her eyes. A pressure cuff squeezed her arm. The medic pulled out a stethoscope and held it against her chest.

As Amber's body began to warm, she began to shake violently.

"I'm going to give her a light sedative," the medic said, holding up a syringe. "It won't knock her out, but she'll feel calmer."

"Look at me, baby. Look at me," Hunter commanded.

Amber stared into Hunter's safe eyes and felt a pinch in her arm. She could feel the medicine traveling up her arm, warming her, making her feel sleepy. Those green eyes. She could swim in them forever.

"You can close your eyes if you want. I'm not going anywhere."

Amber shook her head. She needed to see him, needed to know that she was not going to wake up alone in the shed.

At last, the ambulance stopped. The doors swung open. Everything else after that was a blur. Stained ceiling tiles flashed by over her head. Everyone wore green and rushed.

The lights. Oh, the lights were so bright. And everything was finally so warm. But there were scary things too. Police officers and badges. But the doctors pushed those people away. Hunter?

"Hunter?" she croaked, her voice desperate.

A nurse with kind eyes patted her cheek.

"Let us check you out first, sweetie." The soothing voice floated above her head.

"We'll let you seen him later. I promise."

Amber felt a chill and a sting as someone dabbed at the cut on her temple. The remaining plastic was pulled away. Unseen hands tugged the boots off her feet. Helped her out of her filthy clothes. Dressed her in a soft gown.

So tired. She closed her eyes.

Voices. Hunter's hand squeezing her own. A uniformed officer asking questions. Her voice responding. Sobbing. A nurse asking her to swallow pills. Amber observed it all as if she was dreaming. Eyes heavy. Then nothing.

Soft snoring. A weight on her stomach. Amber opened her eyes and realized she was lying on a hospital bed. Half in a chair and half slumped across her, his head on her belly, Hunter slept. One protective hand rested on top of hers.

She stared at him in wonder. Bits and pieces of the previous night came back to her. The horror of the previous days seemed like a horrible dream. But no, it must have been real. Why else was she here?

She tried to move her free hand, but it was stiff and attached to something. She looked up and saw that she was connected to an IV. She tried to speak, but her throat was still raw. Her eyes grew heavy. She slept again.

Chapter 34

It was morning when she woke again. The IV was gone, but there was a Styrofoam cup on a table by her bed. She vaguely remembered a nurse helping her take sips of juice from it earlier. Hunter was gone. Had she simply imagined him in the night?

She heard a soft click and the door to her room opened. Hunter appeared with a large vase of flowers. He put them on a side table.

"Hey, gorgeous," he said softly. "How do you feel?"

"I love you," Amber whispered. "When I was . . . all alone, I kept thinking that I never told you."

"Oh, baby! I love you, too!"

Hunter leaned over and kissed her gently on the cheek. Were those tears in his eyes?

"When I found out that you were missing, I thought I was going to go insane."

"I don't understand . . ." Amber started to say when there was a knock on the door.

She looked up to see Caleb and Megan's faces pressed against the window.

"If you feel up to it, baby, they really want to see you," Hunter said, squeezing her hand.

"They've been here since we brought you in."

Amber nodded. "It's okay. I'd like to see them."

Hunter gave a thumbs up and Caleb and Megan tumbled into the room.

"Amber, are you really okay? We've been so worried."

Megan and Caleb gave her cautious hugs.

Amber tried to sit up in the bed. "I'm a little achy. But other than that, I feel okay. Except I'm hungry. Do you think they would let me eat something?"

Hunter reached over and pressed a call button for the nurse.

"That should be easy enough to take care of."

Amber studied her friends. "I still don't understand how you guys found me."

Hunter leaned over anxiously. "You don't have to talk about this now."

Amber gave him a wan smile. "It's okay, really. Talking about it means that I won't simply be wondering."

Hunter looked doubtful. But he scooted his chair closer to her and took her hand.

"In that case, Caleb and Megan should start with their end of the story."

The nurse entered and motioned everyone aside.

"What can I get for you, sweetie?"

"Is it okay if I eat? I'm famished."

The nurse checked her watch.

"You're still in time to have breakfast sent up. Let me check your chart and see if the doctor placed any restrictions on what you can have."

Caleb leaned over and whispered in her ear.

"If they don't have decent food, Megan and I will sneak you something later."

The nurse swatted Caleb with Amber's chart.

"I heard that young man. Lucky for you, the doctor said she can have whatever she wants."

The nurse held up a pressure cuff.

"Let me just check your vitals while I'm in here," she said, smiling. "If the doctor clears you later this morning, you can go home this afternoon."

Amber filled out a request for pancakes, bacon, and juice and the nurse took it on the way out.

"Okay, you two start filling me in," she said, motioning for Caleb and Megan to pull chairs up.

"Well, I think you knew that I was picking Caleb up yesterday morning so we could hang out at the park."

Megan's eyes look tired from lack of sleep. Her coppery locks were pulled up in a messy ponytail and stray pieces floated around her face.

"So when I came by to pick him up, I saw a canvas bag in the drive. Seemed a little weird, so I asked Caleb about it before we left."

"I knew you always wore your sneakers to work," Caleb jumped in. "So we figured you put them down and just forgot about them."

"Right," agreed Megan. "So we decided to bring them to the store for you."

"We probably got there not more than a half hour after your shift should have started," Caleb continued. "And that was when things got a little crazy."

"One of your co-workers said that you had gone out to say goodbye to a friend but never came back," Megan said.

Caleb shifted in his chair and took Megan's hand.

"Nobody knew what to think. Your boss said that you were one of her most responsible employees. She knew you wouldn't leaving without telling anyone."

"Hannah lied to me," Amber whispered.

Hunter put a reassuring hand on her shoulder.

"Megan organized a search party for the parking lot. Your manager and coworkers pitched in."

Caleb paused and glanced at Megan. He looked uncomfortable.

"We . . . um . . . We saw a purse on the ground," Megan said. "Caleb recognized it right away."

Hunter's whole body stiffened.

Amber knew he was remembering the details she had given the police.

"It's okay," she said. "It was scary, but it's over now."

Amber looked down at her body to convince herself she was really okay. In spite of everything, she was here with her friends and all in one piece.

Caleb let out a breath and continued. "Your supervisor called the police and I called Hunter. We searched the parking lot for the Range Rover while we waited. But of course it was gone."

Caleb winced and Amber realized how hard that phone call must have been for him. He must have felt at least partially responsible. She suddenly knew that he needed to hear that it wasn't his fault.

"Caleb," she said carefully. "I was really stupid about Hannah. You tried to warn me that something was going on, but I let my ego get in the way."

"Amber, baby, don't," Hunter tried to say.

But Amber squeezed his hand firmly.

"No, let me finish," she said softly, just to him.

Hunter didn't look happy, but he nodded.

"When Hannah sent me the text, I should have immediately been suspicious. The whole time she had been trying to borrow . . ."

Here, Amber paused for a breath and to gather her courage.

"No . . . That's wrong. She was trying to steal the car. I kept telling myself that she would never actually go through with something like that. But the truth was that Hannah hasn't been a true friend for quite some time."

"Amber, really. You don't have to explain to us," Caleb said, his voice anxious.

Amber faced her friends. "But I have to explain to myself. I had a lot of time to think yesterday. This is something I need to say out loud. For my sake."

Megan reached over and patted her hand.

"Say whatever you need to. Just know that you don't have to."

Amber smiled ruefully. "That's why it feels important for me."

She turned and gave Hunter a quick peck on his cheek. "For us."

Hunter bit his lip as though to keep himself from objecting.

Amber was impressed. Hunter must really be struggling with his control freak tendencies right now.

"Even when I saw that there was not another car around that she could have driven, I ignored my instinct. I wanted so hard to believe that she hadn't changed, that she wasn't out to use me."

Amber struggled to keep herself from crying. Her new friends had shown her more love and respect in the last couple of months than Hannah had in years.

"But that was a lie. Even in high school, she used me. I was always her alibi when she went to parties. I would be sitting in the library and she would be getting wasted. Then I came home and lied to the very people who had given me nothing but love."

Amber sniffled.

"Okay, Amber, this is enough," Hunter warned, his voice a growl. "You've been through a traumatic experience and you don't need to do this to yourself. This was not your fault!"

A few hot tears fell down her cheeks. Amber dug her nails into her palms to stop the flow. If she started weeping now, she wasn't sure if she could stop.

She turned and held a finger against Hunter's lips.

"I'm just telling you and Caleb and Megan and myself that Wimpy Amber is gone. I'll never let someone treat me like that again."

"Nobody is ever going to hurt you again, Amber," Hunter said, his green eyes smoldering.

"Not on our watch," Caleb added grimly.

Megan put up a hand and winked at Amber.

"I think Amber gets the point, guys. How about we lower the rage-induced testosterone levels in the room a bit?"

Hunter gaped at the redhead.

But Amber giggled. Megan instinctively knew how to lower the tension in the room. Her comment was perfectly timed.

"Hunter, I don't know how well you know Megan. But you should know she isn't the meek little girl she pretends to be."

Megan laughed. "Hey, don't give away all my secrets!"

Hunter and Caleb visibly relaxed and Amber was glad that Megan had come.

"So how did you track the Range Rover?"

"Oh, that was easy," Caleb said. "Hunter installed a tracking device on it when he first got it."

Amber and Megan stared at Hunter incredulously.

"What? It saves on insurance." Hunter crossed his harms defensively.

"So the police had no trouble tracking your so-called friend and her criminal boyfriend."

Caleb looked like he wanted to punch someone.

"So Hannah told you where I was?" Amber asked, still not understanding.

"No," Hunter said, tightly. "Hannah refused to talk. So did the creep."

"But then how did you find me?"

What was it that nobody seemed to want to tell her?

"You know, I think that Hunter and Amber need some alone time."

Megan stood up and leaned over to give Amber another hug.

"We'll come by and see you at home if you're up to it later."

Amber caught Caleb sending Hunter an apologetic look.

Megan snapped her fingers. "Let's go, Caleb."

Caleb blushed as he hugged Amber. But he looked happy as he followed Megan out the door.

Hunter gaped as the two left the room.

"Did Caleb just allow her to order him around?"

Amber grinned.

"He's like a little puppy trying to please her. I'll tell you about their first meeting later."

"Sound's interesting."

Hunter stared at her with those hypnotic green eyes. He looked nervous.

Amber folded her arms across her chest. She narrowed her eyes at Hunter.

"You want to tell me something?"

Hunter cleared his throat.

"Maybe you should get a little rest first," he said, clearly trying to stall.

Amber shook her head.

"I need to know the rest of the story. Then I can put it behind me. Behind us."

Hunter groaned and ran his hands through his hair.

"I hope you believe that everything I've ever done was to help you."

Amber stared at him.

"Why don't you just start at the beginning from Caleb's phone call," she suggested.

Hunter swallowed and stared at his hands.

"I was with a client when my phone buzzed. I looked down, hoping it was you with one of your silly messages. It was Caleb."

Hunter played with the edge of the sheet.

"Caleb doesn't text me often. And certainly not when he knows I'm working. So I was worried at once. I excused myself and let Isabelle know that there was an emergency."

He grimaced. "Of course I had no idea how bad of an emergency. After Caleb filled me in I got here as fast as a I could. Thank goodness for the company's private jet."

Amber studied him. He was still holding something back. What was he so afraid to tell her?

The edge of the sheet Hunter was fiddling with looked mangled.

"I knew the police could track the Range Rover. But when you weren't with it I nearly had a heart attack. They found the cell phone in the woods. But . . . Well, I knew that I could still help find you."

Amber pulled the sweaty and wrinkled bit of sheet out of his hands.

"Um . . . Are you part bloodhound?" she asked, trying to lighten the mood.

Hunter stared into her eyes.

"Promise me you won't start yelling when I tell you? Please? I want you to be able to go home."

He attempted a smile. "If they come in here and your blood pressure is off the charts, they might say no."

"Tell me, Hunter."

"Promise me, first."

He looked as wistful as a little boy asking for candy.

"I can't promise you I won't be angry."

She forced herself not to melt in those gorgeous eyes.

"You've clearly done something to antagonize me."

Staring into his eyes was a mistake. She felt herself softening.

"But because I'm anxious to get out of here, I promise not to yell."

Hunter grinned.

She reconsidered. "At least until we get home."

Hunter's grin disappeared.

"Fair enough," he said, swallowing hard. "Just remember that I found you."

"Hunter," Amber said through clenched teeth. "Just tell me what you did!"

"I . . . um . . . sort of chipped you."

Chapter 35

"Chipped me? What does that even mean?"

"Well, not you, exactly, but your bracelet. I . . . um . . . Your bracelet has this little chip. A tracking device. That was how we found you."

Amber's mouth fell open.

Hunter leaned forward anxiously.

"Baby, without that . . . I mean . . . I would have turned the whole state upside down looking for you. But it was so cold last night . . ."

Amber stared at her bracelet. Her beautiful, sparkling bracelet was a tracking device? Why?

She started to speak and then simply shut her mouth.

Hunter looked desolate. His green eyes were stormy.

Her wonderful, demented control freak.

What had gone through his mind? Anyone would have panicked. But for a control freak? She couldn't imagine how helpless he must have felt, having to rely on others while he was stuck on another continent.

Demented or not, she had survived thanks to him. Hunter was right. She wasn't sure how long she could have survived in that freezing cold shed. It could have taken days or even weeks to locate her.

"Why?" she asked suddenly.

Hunter stared at her, biting his lip nervously.

"Why what?" He looked startled.

"Why did you put it on the bracelet? What were you thinking when you did it?"

Hunter's eyes watered.

"I was worried about you skipping meals and passing out alone somewhere. I had no idea that something like this could happened."

He rubbed his eyes with his fist. Again he looked like a little boy.

"I know I can be controlling. I'm working on that. But I've wanted to protect you since the first time you collapsed at my feet in front of the art building."

Amber swallowed. She had never seen him so vulnerable before. So raw with emotion. And then she had a revelation.

"Hunter, you didn't fail me when you went to Paris."

"This wouldn't have happened," he said, starting to cry.

"Hunter Webb, you stop this right now," she said firmly, lifting his face.

"Yes, you are a control freak. And we probably need to figure out why that is."

She smiled. "But you are also the nicest control freak I've ever met in my life. I've never had anyone care about me so much."

She scooted over in the bed.

"Now, I know I probably stink to high heaven, but come here. Let me hold you."

Hunter did as she asked, snuggling against her. Then something inside him snapped, and he sobbed against her.

His reaction stunned her. Caught up in her own insecurities, she had never considered that Hunter might have his own issues. What if Hunter's control freak nature was not just some weird idiosyncrasy. Did Hunter have his own scars? Or was she being paranoid?

Hunter sat up and wiped his face, looking sheepish.

"You must think I'm just a big baby."

H reached over her to grab tissues from the bedside table.

"It's okay for big boys to cry," Amber protested.

"I'll just go and wash my face," Hunter said, clearly embarrassed.

Amber listened to him blow his nose loudly in the adjoining bathroom. Then she remembered what she must look and smell like.

She carefully scooted to the edge of the bed and swung her legs off. No dizziness. That was a good sign. She slid off the bed, her feet hitting the cold tile floor. She knocked softly on the bathroom door.

Hunter opened up right away. He must have stuck his whole head in the sink because even his hair was dripping.

"Should you be up yet? Shouldn't we ask the nurse first?"

Amber took one horrified look in the mirror. Her hair was matted and streaked with potting soil. Dried flecks of blood crusted the small gash on her forehead. A big purple bruise covered most of her right shoulder. Her skin was smeared with dirt. She sniffed at her body and made a face. Ugh!

"Nope! I'm getting in the shower right now before anyone can stop me."

Amber turned the shower on.

"Turn your head," she demanded as she slipped out of her hospital gown.

"At least sit on the shower stool," Hunter said, sounding alarmed. "And just a quick rinse. You can bathe when we get home."

Amber ignored him and pumped out a thick gob of soap from the dispenser. The warm water felt heavenly on her skin. Still, she didn't want the nurse to get upset. She lathered her hair and body once, watching in disgust as black rivers of dirt ran down the drain. She rinsed quickly and was already drying off when a nurse knocked on the door.

"Are you okay in there? You should have pushed the call button if you needed to go."

"I'm fine," Amber said in a strong, loud voice. "My boyfriend is making sure I don't fall or anything."

Hunter grinned.

"Okay, sweetie. I'm leaving your breakfast tray. Let me know if you need anything else."

"Thanks!"

Amber didn't want to put on the soiled gown again so she sent Hunter to look for another in the room. He came back a minute later with a huge one.

"Sorry. This was all that was in the drawer. I'll have to go ask for another."

"Better than nothing I suppose," Amber sighed, wrapping the gown around her several times. She looked ridiculous, but at least she felt clean.

By the time Amber finished her pancakes and bacon, Hunter had returned with a smaller gown, a comb, and a toothbrush.

"I sent Caleb a text. He and Megan are bringing clean clothes for you to wear home."

Amber suddenly looked up in alarm. "My boots! Were they able to save those?"

Hunter looked pained.

"Are you sure? I can get you a pair that doesn't remind you of what happened."

Amber was in the middle of removing a particular difficult tangle from her hair. But she shook her head firmly.

"Those boots helped save me," she said. "Unless they're ripped or stained beyond repair, I want to keep them."

Hunter sighed, looking doubtful. "Are you sure that's wise?"

Amber paused, searching for words that would make sense.

"I like to think that it was my own strength and focus that got me through until you found me. And those boots . . . Well, I know it sounds crazy, but those boots gave me hope."

Hunter nodded slowly.

"You were amazing, baby. I didn't want to upset you by talking about it."

"I'm not a psychologist, but I know that talking about stuff always makes it a little easier."

She studied Hunter for a minute.

"When I was younger, I used to squash all my anger against my mom inside me. It was like I was walking around with this huge black pit inside me. But I had this awesome teacher in middle school. She got me to open up and just talk about stuff off the record."

Hunter came over and held her. "I'm sorry, Amber. I'll do whatever you want to do. It's hard for me to talk about because I was so scared. I just want to focus on now."

Amber stroked his face.

"Trust me, Hunter. If you try to push everything away, it will just pop up somewhere later. Either in your dreams or in your . . ."

Amber broke off. She was going to say *in your behavior*. Hmm . . . Now she really wanted to know if there was something in Hunter's past.

"Okay. Okay. I can accept that you need to talk about it. But not this minute, okay?" he pleaded.

Amber grinned mischievously. "How about I postpone the conversation in return for my boots?"

Hunter frowned. "This isn't a funny topic, Amber."

Amber stuck her tongue out at him. "You deal with your fright your way. I'll deal with mine how I want to."

She looked him in the eye.

"Seriously, Hunter, I learned a long time ago that humor was a great coping technique. That's how I've managed so much craziness this far in life."

Hunter grinned slyly.

"Fine. But I'm going to come up with my own coping mechanism."

Amber stared at him curiously. "So you plan to cope how?"

Hunter traced her lips with his finger.

"A little mouth to mouth might help," he whispered.

Amber blushed. "Is that a promise?"

Hunter stared at her with clear longing.

"Gorgeous, that's a guarantee!"

Hunter bent to kiss her.

A loud knock on the door startled them both.

A doctor with a clipboard stood in the doorway.

"Well, Miss Holloway, I'm certainly glad to see that you are feeling refreshed enough to . . . ah . . . engage in some pleasantries."

Amber blushed.

"I was just providing oxygen," Hunter said with a straight face.

The doctor winked. She looked like she was having trouble not laughing.

"I doubt that Miss Holloway's injuries require mouth to mouth resuscitation. But it's good to know that you're on top of things. I take it you'll be responsible for taking care of our patient once I release her?"

"Yes, ma'am," Hunter said, his face serious now. "Just tell me what I should do."

The doctor checked over Amber's bruises and shone a light in her eyes.

"You're a smart young woman. Wrapping that plastic around you kept you from getting hypothermia."

The doctor checked her pulse and listened to her heart.

"Any dizziness today? Blurred vision? Headache?"

Amber shook her head to each question.

"Then I think that you are all set to go home. If anything changes, let us know."

Hunter pumped his fists in the air after the doctor left the room.

"Let's get you out of this joint!"

Chapter 36

Amber felt as though she was in a dream. The past couple of days had gone by in a blur as Hunter scrambled to help her secure a passport and a ticket to Paris. He claimed that it was no big deal, but she wondered just how much it had cost and how much his family connections had helped.

She still couldn't believe that she was sitting in a private service car being shuttled to the airport. This was her first real taste of what life was like for the wealthy.

Prior to this, Amber's only experience with flying was a lone school trip to the state capital. She remembered sitting on the floor in the airport terminal with a group of rowdy teens after their flight got delayed for more than five hours. She had slept on top of her duffel bag, wedged between several other classmates. She had gotten to the airport by bus.

Hunter reached over and put a hand on her knee.

"Is everything okay?"

Amber smiled. "I was just remembering my last trip to the airport. It wasn't quite this fancy."

"No beverages? No snacks?" Hunter took a sip of his soda.

"Well, I was offered a fried chicken leg by the woman sitting beside me. But the ambiance was a bit different."

She sniffed the air. "I mean, where is the smell of fuel?"

"Train? Subway? Bus?" Hunter quizzed, raising his eyebrows.

"What was this delightful mode of transport?"

Amber laughed. "Our city's finest local bus, complete with the crankiest driver known on the planet."

Hunter sighed and nuzzled her shoulder with his chin.

"Ah, and here I am disappointing you with our car service. I'm afraid that Edward is most annoyingly calm and courteous. And it appears as though the interior has been cleaned recently."

Hunter paused, lifted his chin, and sniffed the air. He shook his head dismally.

"I'm afraid that there isn't a trace of bus fuel to amuse you."

Amber giggled as she stared into Hunter's beautiful green eyes. Reaching up, she pushed a lock of dark hair from his forehead. She would never get tired of those eyes.

"I think you need a hair cut," she murmured, enjoying the closeness and solitude that the car provided.

"Hmm ... You're probably right. I was going to get one this week but ..."

Hunter broke off, looking anxious.

Amber reached up and stroked his cheek.

"It's okay to mention that I had a bad couple of days."

Hunter kissed her lightly on the forehead.

"You know how I feel about that," he said, but his tone was soft and casual.

Amber knew that Hunter still blamed himself for the incident on New Year's Eve. She constantly reminded him that there was absolutely nothing that he could have done to prevent it. In fact, it was only due to his overly protective, control freak nature that she was sitting here safe and sound.

"It's amazing how wound up people can get over a simple little kidnapping," she said lightly, watching Hunter's face carefully.

Hunter's eyes widened and he scowled at her.

"You know how I feel about you joking about it," he said angrily.

Amber tightened beside him.

"And you know how I feel about not joking about it," she said, her tone equally sore.

"If I'm going to put this behind me, I need to feel in control."

Hunter held up his hand, instantly looking apologetic.

"I'm sorry, Amber. This is still so hard for me." He smiled ruefully.

"I am trying," he said softly. "I know it might not appear like it on the surface but . . ."

Amber put a finger on his lips.

"It's okay. I get it. I know how you are. But we have to be willing to talk about everything. Both the good and the bad if we want to make this relationship . . ."

She broke off, horrified that she had used the "r" word.

To her surprise, Hunter smiled.

"So you agree that we have a relationship to work on?"

"Well, yes," she said, blushing.

"Even though I'm a control freak?"

Amber laughed. "Yes. Even though you are an absolute, certified, raging control freak."

"Well, I do pride myself on doing things well."

Amber groaned. "So now who's using jokes to avoid the issue at hand?"

Hunter laughed.

"Hey, I learn from the best!"

"You know we're going to have to talk about these issues at some point," Amber warned.

"Okay! I get it. But not today. Today is all about taking my girl to one of the most romantic cities on the planet."

Hunter pouted and traced a finger along her chin.

"Can't you just give me a little break from analyzing my messed up tendencies?"

"Hmm . . . Let me think about that," Amber said, smiling mischievously.

"I might be persuaded to forget about certain things with a kiss or two."

"That sounds like a bargain price," Hunter murmured, moving closer and bringing his lips to her ear.

Amber shivered as his warm breath hit her neck.

"How about I start the first one here?" Hunter lightly grazed Amber's earlobe with his lips.

"Um . . . Okay. That's a good start."

Hunter moved and kissed her cheek. "And that one?"

"Keep going," Amber said, smiling.

Hunter kissed the tip of her nose. "How about that one?"

"I'll give you another try," Amber said, staring into Hunter's eyes.

Finally, Hunter nipped her bottom lip gently before capturing it between his own lips. He kissed her deeply.

Amber kept her eyes open, swimming in the green, stormy sea of Hunter's eyes. When he finally pulled away, she had to catch her breath. She needed to pinch herself.

Amber Holloway, how did you get so lucky?

Amazing. She was jetting off to Paris with the man of her dreams.

****

**Want to read the conclusion to
Hunter and Amber's story?**
Start reading *Love is Beautiful Book 2*

Visit elliejadamsauthor.com for a complete
list of Sweet Romance books by Ellie.

Newsletter

Join my Newsletter and receive a Sweet Romance story as my gift to you. You will also receive author updates, new release alerts, and exclusive contests and discounts. Free to Join. No Spam. Unsubscribe Anytime. Join at www.elliejadamsauthor.com

Books by Ellie J. Adams

For a complete list of my Sweet Romance books, visit:
www.elliejadamsauthor.com

About the Author

247

Ellie J. Adams's books have been downloaded over half-a-million times by readers around the world. She is a romantic at heart and likes her characters to find their Happily Ever After. Ellie's books offer moments of drama, humor, and heartache along the way. Her leading men are strong, but flawed, males, and the leading women are sweet, smart, and independent. Ellie writes sweet romance you can get swept up in and takes you away.